The Kennedy Rifle

JK Brandon

www.jkbrandon.com

The Kennedy Rifle copyright © 2011 by Jerry Brandon

Cover art copyright © 2011 by Jerry Brandon

ISBN-13: 978-1468145809
ISBN-10: 1468145800

All rights reserved.

This is a work of fiction. Names, characters, places and incidents are either the product of the author's imagination or are used fictitiously. Any resemblance to actual persons living or dead, businesses, companies, events or locales is entirely coincidental. All rights reserved. No part of this publication may be reproduced or transmitted in in any form or by any means, electronic or mechanical, without permission in writing from Jerry Brandon

"The only thing necessary for the triumph of evil—is for good men to do nothing."

—John Fitzgerald Kennedy, 1961 speech, quoting Sir Edmund Burke

PROLOGUE

NOVEMBER 22, 1963

It would be difficult to find a better spot to shoot the President.

From their concealed vantage point on the top of the hill, the two assassins can view the entire plaza but remain undetected until the moment of fire. The Presidential motorcade will enter Dealey Plaza on Houston Street, make a wide, slow turn onto Elm in front of the Texas School Book Depository, then proceed past the base of the grassy knoll.

They stand in back of a weathered split-rail fence, pacing and smoking cigarettes. Some rain fell this November early morning, and the muddy earth captures their impatience. They arrived at noon with means and motive, now they wait for opportunity. A short rifle case leans against the fence by their feet.

Behind them is a large parking area with a few parked cars. Behind that sits a train yard and a railroad tower. The railroad dispatcher in the tower noticed some unusual activity around noon, but reported nothing to authorities. A car circled the lot several times before dropping the two men off.

Groups of spectators dot the hill in front of the fence, but the assassins are not concerned about being seen. Dense trees line the fence, and men in suits with Secret Service badges keep people from getting too close. Men in suits are not unusual in 1963, even in Dallas, Texas.

The knoll assassin looks at his watch, 12:20. Sixty feet away, businessman Abraham Zapruder stands on a short concrete wall holding an 8mm movie camera. He will film the President's car as it drives by. In eleven minutes, Zapruder will get down from the wall, call the local FBI and tell them he has just recorded the assassination of President John F. Kennedy.

The knoll gunman removes an unusual weapon from the rifle case. He is one of three shooters waiting, two others hide in tall buildings lining the plaza caravan route.

At 12:22 a commotion erupts in the plaza as a man suffers an epileptic seizure. The crowd on the hill moves toward the man, away from the two assassins. An ambulance arrives instantly to take the man away. At the base of the grassy knoll, a man in a suit stands holding an unopened black umbrella. The sun shines brightly.

At 12:25 the knoll shooter and his spotter are in position with their rifle barrel resting on the top of the fence. JFK's motorcade is due any moment. Lee Harvey Oswald sits alone in the second-floor lunchroom of the Texas School Book Depository, four floors below what will later be called the Sniper's Nest.

At 12:30 the President's limousine enters Dealey Plaza on Houston and drives toward the School Book Depository. John and Jackie sit in the rear of the convertible, Texas Governor John Connally and his wife are in the middle seat. From the supposed Oswald window sniper's nest, the best shot is now, firing at the approaching motorcade. No shot is taken.

The motorcade makes the slow turn onto Elm, driving toward the grassy knoll at eleven miles per hour. The DalTex building stands next to the Book Depository and is behind the President's limo. The man with the black umbrella opens it and holds it over his head.

A shot fires from the DalTex building second-floor window, striking the pavement directly behind the limousine, missing even the car. Kennedy stops waving and turns his head as the gun cracks. Governor Connally looks to his right at the sound.

Ahead on the knoll, the rifleman has the President in his sights. He squeezes off a shot. It strikes dead center but low, passing thru six layers of silk tie knot. Even with its velocity greatly reduced, the bullet still pierces Kennedy's windpipe. The President grabs at his throat with both hands, fighting to draw a breath.

A third shot rings out, from the School Book Depository now, barely missing the President. It slams into Governor Connally's back, penetrating his right armpit and exiting close to his right nipple.

The Secret Service has yet to react. Kennedy's limousine continues closer to the grassy knoll.

Now a fourth shot is fired, this one from the knoll, missing the President but ricocheting off the limo. Simultaneously the fifth shot comes from the DalTex building third-floor window. It is the second shot to hit the President. The force of a large-caliber bullet drives JFK forward, but his stiff back-brace holds him upright. Secret Service agents look over at the President but do not react. The limousine slows further as it passes the base of the knoll. The man with the black umbrella pumps it up and down. The spotter behind the fence knows they can wait no longer. In a few seconds Jackie Kennedy will be in the line of fire. The limo is barely moving, its driver turns around to look at the President. John Kennedy is wounded but not fatally.

The spotter calls for the kill shot.

From the grassy knoll, shot number six explodes into JFK's temple, ripping a swath through his brain and blowing out a skull chunk the size of a baseball. A motorcycle officer riding behind is struck in the face with a sheet of blood and brain tissue. Skull fragments fly thirty-feet to the rear and side of the limo as the President's brain is completely exposed. A fine red mist rains on the car's occupants.

Six-tenths of a second later, shot number seven hits Governor Connally in the wrist and then his thigh. This shot comes from the Book Depository sixth floor, but on the opposite side from the Oswald window.

Finally the limousine accelerates away, a Secret Service agent desperately shielding the President's limp body.

Behind the grassy knoll fence, the assassins place their weapon in the case and calmly walk away.

CHAPTER ONE

PRESENT DAY

It was hard to tell with the blood in his eyes, but it looked like the water-stained ceiling in his office, which meant he was flat on his back, and that concerned him a little, since prone was not his normal position at work, at least not before lunch.

Michael Cole remembered a few things; a heated argument, a black handgun and something about a woman named Kate. That first part was no surprise, he had a knack for pissing people off. The gun part was no big deal either, he owned a few. But the woman, who the hell was she?

He wiped one eye and tried to break through the fog of what just happened. If only—

Oof!

Reality returned with a kick to his ribs. He curled up from the pain and rolled on his side.

Oh yeah. I'm getting my ass kicked.

He squinted and saw blood on the carpet, four black boots, and the business end of a Glock nine mil. One of the men bent over Cole's face.

"You got it, now?"

The guy was convincing, to be sure. He had the handgun, the other man had the muscles. So far they'd only used the muscle. It seemed like they wanted something and he wasn't cooperating. But what was it?

Cole tried the truth. "Got *what?*"

Oof!

He clenched his teeth, rolled the other way and took a mental inventory of body parts. They hadn't hurt him too bad yet, but he was afraid they might before it was over. What he needed was a minute to clear his head. He gestured toward the other room.

"Water."

The pistolero backed off, stuffed the gun in his sagging pants and crossed tattooed arms.

"Chow, get him a drink."

Chow shuffled into the office lunchroom to find a glass. They were accommodating, if nothing else. When the water arrived, Cole sat up on the floor and leaned against the couch. He drank half in one pull and considered the situation.

The first guy was a flyweight Hispanic sporting an earring, a Glock and a bad attitude. Cole wasn't worried about him, he was just a mouth waving a gun. But friend Chow seemed treacherous with his perfectly-round, shaved-head bolted directly to immense shoulders. He looked to be an ethnic mix, maybe half-Asian and half-Rottweiler. He was wide and thick and hard, like you could lay into him with a baseball bat and it would just piss him off.

They seemed more like L.A. trouble than Phoenix boys.

Cole dabbed at the trickle of blood over his eye, grateful that nothing was broken.

He wiped his mouth with the back of his hand. "You guys look like you're new in town. Let me give you some advice." Cole held up his glass of water. "Phoenix is actually a desert, you need to stay hydrated."

He remembered now. *Stay away from Kate Marlowe.*

Don't even talk to her. Except he wasn't. He'd never heard of Kate Marlowe. No clue. They didn't believe him, the last time he told them the lights went out.

Somehow he'd rattled the wrong cage.

He tried to push back to see if they'd give up more info. If he was going to be told what to do, he wanted to know who was giving the orders. Cole nodded at big and dumb.

"Chow doesn't say much, does he?"

Skinny played with his pistol. "Maybe he don't like you."

For a minute nobody spoke. Cole stared at Chow. "Cat got your tongue?"

Chow gave him a sick grin, then opened his mouth wide to reveal a ragged stump where his tongue should be.

Cole cleared his throat.

A file cabinet across the room sat with its drawer's half-open, its files scattered. What wasn't thrown on the floor was out of place, what wasn't out of place was broken.

He tried again. "I'm telling you, she hasn't been here. I don't know who this woman is. You guys sure you got the right address?"

Skinny pointed the Glock sideways like some punk-ass homeboy.

"This Bowlistic FX?"

"Ballistic Effects."

"What?"

"It's pronounced Ballistic Effects, Not Bowlistic F, X."

Skinny dug a piece of paper out of his pocket and glanced at it. "Whatever, man."

"Anything else?" Cole asked.

"Are you Mister Michael Cole, the famous Bowlistic expert?"

"Ballistic."

"What?"

"Yes, I'm Michael Cole."

"This Phoenix, Arizona?"

"Technically, this is Scottsdale, Arizona."

Skinny looked at Chow, then back at Cole.

"Scottsdale, Phoenix, what the hell's the difference?"

"For one thing, the bars charge more."

Cole hoped they'd make their point and leave, but it looked like they were enjoying themselves too much. So far it was only threats and bruises, but a gun-in-your-face was still a gun-in-your-face, even if it was a sideways nine-millimeter.

"OK, Mister Cole. You say she ain't been here yet, that's fine. But she shows up, you don't do no work for her. Got it?"

"Not even for cash?"

Skinny lunged forward and grabbed Cole by shirt. His spittle punctuated his threats. "Listen gabacho. You startin' to piss me off, how 'bout my friend here carve his initials on your forehead?"

Cole cocked his head. "Chow can spell?"

Probably shouldn't have said that.

He squirmed as Chow thumbed open a huge folding lockback. Huge. Chow held it up as he stepped forward.

Enough of this. Cole needed to get his gun out fast. He visualized every movement of the shot. The smooth presentation, the thumb safety flicked down as the .45 came up quickly, the slow but deliberate trigger squeeze at center mass—once, twice—then a blur over to contestant number two to decide if he lives or dies. Two seconds, maybe one and a half.

Except...he didn't have his gun.

Cole kept his eyes on the tip of the knife.

Think.

If he couldn't shoot them, maybe he could bribe them.

"You guys missed the safe."

Chow stopped moving and stared at him.

"I've got a safe."

"Now you're talking." Skinny relaxed his stance. "Chow, whacha think?"

Chow folded his knife and put it away. Maybe the big guy wasn't so dumb after all.

"Safe. Ain't that nice. Why don't you show us where it is, mister bowlistic expert."

Cole went over to the file cabinet and muscled it sideways three feet, then pulled back a flap of carpet covering a floor-safe set in the concrete.

Skinny waved his pistol. "So open it up, bro. We ain't no safecrackers."

Cole spun the dial left and right until it clicked, but as he lifted the door he felt a gun barrel in his ear.

"Back off, chump. We got this action."

Cole got out of the way as Chow bent down, opened the safe door and removed the contents.

Skinny examined each item as it came out. "Lemme see. We got a nice leather holster here, 100% cowhide, but it don't fit my Glock." He threw it to the side and took the next items. "Now we got some paperwork. Here's an Arizona license for somethin', and we got an Arizona truck title, no lien, and this looks like some divorce papers—that's a shame. Bitch ran off, huh? And an official honorable discharge from the United States Army. So our bowlistic expert was a soldier boy. Great. So, far, ain't nothin' here we want. Then we got us two new boxes .45 ACP ammo—not my style." He set those down gingerly.

Chow handed him up some green bills.

"Whoa, whazziz? One, two, three...five! Five fresh one-hundred dollar bills!" He stuffed those in his pants.

"Lunch money, damn. Thank you very much. What else he got, Chow?"

Chow stood up and spread his hands.

Cole spoke up. "Look, I get the message. I won't work for Kate Marlowe. *You* don't like her, *I* don't like her."

"That's right. 'Cause we hear you do, we'll come back and mess you up good."

Cole rubbed his temples with both hands. "Messed up good. Got it."

They seemed satisfied with their damage and his submission. Skinny cackled on his way out the door. "Tell the maid we're sorry for the mess."

Cole rose on wobbly legs to lock the front door behind them, then walked slowly to the bathroom mirror to see what a careless victim of violent crime looked like. It wasn't pretty. The good news was he wouldn't need stitches, just bandages. The bloody gash on his forehead was down to a slow weep, he had a multi-colored bruise on his right cheek and a raised welt on the left.

He leaned forward and washed his face with soap and hot water, then splashed cold water on it over and over, letting the pink water drip back in the sink. Finally he raised his head and stared at himself in the mirror.

Idiot.

Cole opened a new first-aid kit and used the cream, gauze pads and adhesive tape for best effect. The result was successful but guaranteed to scare small dogs and children. He didn't give a damn.

Cole took a few deep breaths and probed his ribs; they were painful to the touch but not broken. He peeled off his shirt and dropped it in the corner. He took a moment to admire the purple bruises on his torso, then walked back in the office.

The bottom desk drawer held a stack of clean polo shirts. He pulled a black one over his head carefully, thinking again about the two men who just left. He was still in the dark about what just happened, but he wouldn't let it happen again.

Idiot.

Cole opened a file box on a closet shelf and retrieved his HK45 and kydex holster. He dropped the magazine and checked, it was full of 230 grain ball. He chambered a round and flipped the safety on. The holster clipped to his belt behind his right hip.

The front office windows rattled as a small private jet landed two blocks away. He didn't look up, jet traffic was not unusual here. Cole leased the small office in the Scottsdale Airpark because it was cheap, not quiet. The noise in this part of Scottsdale didn't bother him as much as all the idiots with money.

Cole scanned the mess around him and then went to work. He stood the file cabinet up and gathered the files in a pile, thinking he could sort them later. He put the picture of his father and his Army stint back on his desk.

He fought rising nausea for a moment, then sat down in his chair to wait for it to subside. The nausea took him back, way back to fourth grade at Our Lady of Perpetual Help.

Lunch was over and the long tables were all cleaned up, but little Michael Cole was still sitting in his chair staring at a solitary glass of tomato juice. *You'll sit there until you finish it all*, Sister said. Hours passed. Bells rang. Classes changed. Flies buzzed all around his head in the deserted lunchroom. The tomato juice turned warmer and more disgusting. Michael crossed his arms and stared anywhere but at the lumpy red glass, fighting the sick feeling in the pit of his stomach. Finally, at ten minutes to three, Emilio the janitor came in the door and pushed his broom slowly around the floor. He paused behind Michael's chair, scooped up the glass of tomato juice and drank it all in one pull. Emilio set the glass down quietly, winked at Michael and kept brooming.

When he felt better, Cole went to the little office refrigerator for something cold and wet. He stared at the contents a while, finally grabbed two bottles of Dos Equis. A little rummaging in desk drawers produced an opener and a bottle of aspirin. He swallowed four tablets with half a beer, then held a cold bottle against each temple.

The front door rattled again. This time it was someone shaking it, and finally knocking. Cole put one hand on his gun and walked to the window and peered thru the blinds. A woman stood waiting. Blonde hair and long legs was all he could see. That was enough.

What the hell, it must be his day for surprises. He scanned the parking lot to see if anyone was watching, then he opened the door. She came in with the April morning breeze.

The blonde took a step backward, then spoke with a slight Texas drawl. "What happened to you?"

He stared at her a moment. "You must be Kate Marlowe."

"And you gotta be Michael Cole," she said.

He sighed. "You're late."

CHAPTER TWO

Cole invited her to sit on the couch while he sat in the chair. She glanced at the papers and books on the floor, then back at him.

He waved a hand in dismissal. "The housekeeper quit."

Kate nodded. "She'll be missed."

Kate Marlowe could have been a college cheerleader a few decades earlier, except for her height. At five-ten she was an inch under Cole. Her facial beauty was honest and natural, unaltered by surgeons or diminished by her few honest lines.

She eyed the beer bottles on the table. "Happy hour already?"

"Those are purely medicinal. Topical application, mostly. Would you like a cold one?"

"No thanks. What happened to you?"

" 'You' happened to me. Two guys came by and tried to convince me not to talk to Kate Marlowe."

If that surprised her at all, she didn't show it. She glanced at the blood spot on the carpet then looked away. "So why did you let me in?"

"Flawed personality. I'm attracted to trouble. You seem to qualify."

She smoothed her hair back with one hand and gave a faint smile. "I'm not usually thought of that way."

"So, how do they think of you?"

"People consider me a nice girl. Most of them, anyway."

He analyzed that. "Leaving some wiggle room?"

The faint smile again. "Wiggling can be fun. But I try not to be trouble."

"Somebody must think you're a problem."

"My ex-husband, for one," she said. "Perhaps a few gentlemen's wives along the way." She leaned back on the couch.

Kate's white silk blouse was tailored modestly, but it struggled to conceal rare natural phenomena. Cole struggled not to look.

He asked, "Are you from the area?"

"Why? Thinking of warning the natives?"

"Seems like the prudent thing to do."

She had a friendly laugh to go with her face. "I'm from Houston."

"Scottsdale vacation?"

"I came to see Michael Cole."

"I'm flattered." He touched his face. "I think."

"My apologies for the outcome. Does this happen to you often?"

"Only when your name is mentioned."

"Who were those two guys?" she asked.

"I was hoping you could tell me that."

"Sorry. I wish I could help you," she said.

Cole let it drop. "How'd you get my name?"

"I was referred to you by several people. The Dallas police, for one."

Interesting.

"In regard to what?"

"Your book. *The Shot from the Knoll.*"

He paused. "This is about Kennedy? That book was three years ago."

"My uncle said you got it right."

Cole snorted. "One of the few."

"He would know. He was there, like your father."

Cole sat speechless. He'd hoped this topic had died. "What do you know about my father?"

"I heard he was in Dallas, at Dealey Plaza that day," she said.

"Who told you that?"

"I think it was the Dallas police, can't remember now."

"Did you know somebody shot him?" Cole asked.

"No. There's a lot I don't know."

"So you're here to talk about the assassination?"

She set her purse in her lap. "Actually, I want to hire you. I have assassination details I want you to examine."

Cole took a long breath. "To what end?"

"To prove it wasn't Oswald. To prove it actually was a conspiracy."

He stared at her. "So you come here to see me, and after all this time, you think we're going to prove it wasn't a lone nut. That there really was a conspiracy to kill John F. Kennedy."

"Isn't that what you believe?"

"I believe it, apparently you believe it. Let's say half the world believes it. Washington will never admit the Presidency changed in a coup so what's the point?"

"The point? Proving the truth."

"Truth is not what we prove, the truth is what they say it is."

"Truth is absolute," she said.

"Only in a just society," he spat the words.

"Gad, you're cynical."

"There's some truth for you."

Silence hung awkwardly in the room. Finally Cole spoke, more out of courtesy than curiosity. He didn't want to cover this ground again. "You said your uncle was there. In Dallas."

She hesitated, then blurted it out. "My uncle worked for the men who killed Kennedy. He was bodyguard for the shooter on the Grassy Knoll."

Cole jumped up. "Now you come forward? Why show-up now when it's too late?"

"It's not too late."

"Yes it is. No one cares."

She spoke with an edge of anger. "Look at your face, somebody cares."

"That doesn't prove anything."

"My uncle was proof. But he's dead. He died three weeks ago and left me to tell the world the truth. But I need your help."

Cole walked around the room. "I'm sorry for your loss, but there's no way to determine who killed Kennedy."

"What if there was, would you be interested?"

He hesitated. "No."

"That's a lie if I ever heard one," she said. "Everyone wants to know the truth."

"I'm sure they do. But it's impossible now. The water's been muddied with lies and half-truths so much it's impossible to sort it out."

She let him cool off, then spoke. "You have some history with this, I understand."

"Some bad history. The Kennedy assassination brought nothing but grief to my family."

She studied him, as if deciding to continue. "What if we could come up with the murder weapon?"

"Meaning what?"

"What if we could produce the real Kennedy rifle? Not Oswald's rifle, but the Grassy Knoll rifle."

She had his attention now. "What do you know about a rifle?" he asked.

"I know where it is. I just need your help to find it."

Cole felt himself falling down a black hole. "I don't believe it."

"Please, I'm not lying. I know where it is."

"Why me?"

"You're a ballistic expert, you can authenticate the rifle. You know all the assassination details."

"I'm not the only guy in America who knows this stuff."

"But you wrote the book on it. The shooter on the knoll, the rifle that would have been used. You've got a good head start."

He shook his head. "I'm sorry. I can't get involved."

"Don't be selfish, this is history making. We've got a chance here."

Cole knew she was right. But something felt wrong. "Who'd your uncle work for?" he asked.

"He was a low-level criminal. I don't know who ordered the hit, but it filtered down to him. Some of the guys he worked with were in the Mafia, some of them worked for CIA fringe people."

"I need more than that."

She hesitated. "Look. I'm not proud of this, it's just what is. My uncle was the driver and bodyguard for Carlos Marcello's hitman. Before that he was involved in training Cubans for the Bay of Pigs invasion. He thought John Kennedy had been responsible for its failure. No aircover, no troops. He had no love for JFK. So when his boss said they were going to kill Kennedy, he was all in. He didn't ask why or who wanted it done."

"You're saying the Mafia killed Kennedy. Or are you saying the CIA?"

"No, I think it was Marcello's decision. My uncle didn't know who wanted it. It just gets handed down the line, you don't know how high-up it goes."

Cole nodded. "It always gets down to a guy with a gun." He sat down and held a cold beer to his temple. The ache was getting worse.

She waited for him to speak, then finally asked. "Will you do it?"

He sighed. "You had me at Kennedy rifle."

She just smiled.

"What do you want me to do?" he asked.

"First off, come to Dallas, come with me to Dealey Plaza."

"Just like that."

She reached in her purse and removed an envelope. "I have two American Airline tickets leaving Sky Harbor at 7am tomorrow morning. We can talk about it on the way, take a look at the Plaza and the Grassy Knoll close up. If you don't want anything to do with it after that, you've only lost a day and a half."

"Yes, but I—"

"I'll pay you for it."

"It's not the money. I have a work-related deposition in two days."

"You can be back in time for that."

He considered. "That's fair."

She handed him a plane ticket. "I'll meet you there in the morning. Don't be late. It'll be worth it."

As she walked to the door, her black skirt pulled tight on her thighs. She paused on the way out. "I have to admit, I did lie about one thing."

"And what was that?"

"I can be a lot of trouble."

***

After she left, Cole sat and considered the wisdom of his decision. Maybe the beating had fogged his brain. Perhaps this wasn't such a good idea after all. What he needed was a second opinion. He locked the office and headed out to his vehicle.

Susan.

He'd go see his older sister, he needed her blunt assessment—or maybe her approval, he wasn't sure. He pulled out of the parking lot and headed north, driving past subdivision after subdivision.

A sea of red-tile roofs stretched for miles in all directions. Developers bladed-off desert hills, filled in the washes and threw up 3.2 houses per acre. Front yards got two inches of crushed granite and a couple Mesquite trees to prove you hadn't bought a house in California after all.

Disney Desert, he thought. Just like his neighborhood.

Her street looked deserted, commuters working, housewives shopping, kids at school. The only sounds were leaf blowers wielded by recent immigrants. He parked in her drive and rang the bell until an early-forties brunette appeared. She looked like him, friends said.

Just better looking.

"Hi sis."

She held a hand over her mouth. "What happened?"

"I got in a fight."

"You're a mess."

"You should see the other guy's boot."

She motioned to him. "Come inside. Did you go to the hospital?"

He stepped in the foyer. "I'm fine, I just came to talk."

She glanced at the gun on his hip, then cocked her head. "You're carrying again?"

"It's necessary, that's all I can say."

"Michael, what's wrong?"

"Nothing, I just need your advice."

"Since when do you take my advice?" she asked

"I'm looking into the Kennedy assassination again."

She put one hand on her hip. She didn't need to say more than that, but she did. "You don't need advice, you need therapy."

"This time it's different."

"Sure it is. Michael, don't be a fool. There's nothing more to find, it's all history now."

"I'm going to visit Dealey Plaza, then hopefully look at physical evidence of the shooting from the grassy knoll."

"What's next, the Roswell UFO crash?"

Cole didn't smile. "So you still think it was Oswald?"

"No. I think the butler did it."

The more she tried to talk him out of it, the better his decision sounded. "I met someone with new information."

"You're finally rebuilding your reputation after the last mess. You can't afford to screw up now." She stewed a minute, and then grilled him for more. "What's so special about this new information?"

"I had a client come to see me. She says her uncle was one of the men on the grassy knoll. One of the assassins."

"She?"

"A woman."

She raised an eyebrow. "Does this woman have red hair?"

"She knows where the knoll rifle is. I know it sounds crazy, but it makes sense. After all this time, something had to come out."

"Crazy is the telling word. Let's say you do find something new. Do you think the papers will print anything about the assassination now? You think you'll hear it on CNN?"

"The fiftieth anniversary is coming up; I think there's going to be a lot of interest. This may be our last chance."

She looked him over like the mother hen she was. "You look tense. When's the last time you got laid? That's what this is about, isn't it? No woman in your life."

"Women and I—"

"You need to meet someone normal and settle down," she said. "Whatever happened to that nice girl, Amy?"

"She met a nice guy. Look, what do you think?"

"For one, I think you should date girls closer to your age."

"Seriously," he said.

"Forget John Kennedy. Have some dinner with us. We're having fried chicken tonight, we've got plenty."

"Thanks, but I'm too wired to eat. Tell me, what do you think dad would think?"

"Dad? I'm not sure." Her eyes softened as she touched his cheek. "Why don't you ask him?"

***

Cole drove north on Scottsdale Road, weaving through the late-afternoon traffic toward the bordering city of Carefree. Just outside of town, he stopped at a small plot of land covered with Mesquite trees bursting with spring leaves. He parked at the side of the road, turned off the ignition and rested his head on the steering wheel. Finally he looked up, removed the pistol from his belt and placed it under the seat.

He strode past small headstones and markers, stopping at a simple grave. Cole stood somberly in front of his father's resting place, communicating silently about the changes in his life.

He couldn't keep his promise about killing. He would defend himself and others, he would do what was necessary.

He needed one more look into the assassination. He didn't know if it would bring more shame to the family, but he had to take this chance.

He stood there; thinking of his last conversation with his father, a man he'd never really known.

I wish we'd had more time.

A light wind rustled through trees scattered throughout the cemetery. The swish and murmur of thin green leaves was comforting, almost like spirits whispering. Cole listened intently. When his father finally gave his blessing, Cole drove home to pack a bag.

CHAPTER THREE

Robert Ryker turned the collar up on his rain coat and left his driver to park the big Audi sedan. A stiff Atlantic breeze drove the rain, stinging his cheek. Ryker didn't notice, he was thinking about the Arizona problem.

He took the dozen steps up to the wharf at Fells Point. He moved slowly but steadily, his progress impeded by a weak left leg but aided by his cane. A half-block later he ducked into Bowmans. The restaurant was normally full with tourists on its crab deck, but this day sat nearly empty. Even the surly waiters looked pleased to see a customer. He hung his raincoat by the bar and took a booth overlooking the water and the gray Baltimore sky.

Ryker pushed a handkerchief through his silver-grey hair, then patted his leathered face dry. He picked up a menu, but dropped it when a waiter appeared.

"Bloody Mary."

The waiter bowed and retreated. Ryker thought alcohol might improve his mood, but he was there for a meeting, not a drink. When the waiter returned, he drank half immediately. He relaxed but kept one eye trained on the door.

The wind pushed the rain against the window in sheets, bending and distorting his view of the harbor, and then of the tall figure who walked past. Ryker thought it must be his man.

The figure shook the rain off his umbrella, then paused for a slow look around the room. Ryker raised his hand and the man came over and slid in the booth. He was tall, thin and blued-eyed, Scandinavian. He took the opposite seat. Ryker only knew him as Neils.

The visitor declined a drink and got right to business. "I brought you a list of our needs," he said.

"Destination?"

"We can arrange pickup."

Ryker shook his head. "I need to know the end-user before I sell anything." He preferred to deal with rebel groups over terrorists. It wasn't a question of ethics, he hoped to avoid the backlash heat.

Neils hesitated. "I represent a Hindu fundamentalist group, the Ananda Marga."

Ryker knew who they were. The Ananda Marga was a constant but minor thorn in the side of the Indian government. The main casualties of their resistance were a few government buildings.

Neils unfolded a single typewritten sheet and passed it to Ryker. He scanned the first items. Three-hundred Kalashnikov folding-stock AK-47's, 20,000 rounds 7.62x39, one-hundred nine-millimeter pistols with 5000 rounds.

Ryker looked up. I can get you Bulgarian Makarov nines, from Arsenal. You'll want their AK's, too. They make the best Kalashnikovs in the world. Chrome bore, plastic furniture, very-well made.

Neils seemed to approve. "And the sniper rifles?"

Ryker looked at the last item on the list. "Druganovs. Top notch. You can have night-sights if you need them. What are you going to use to transport?"

"We have access to an Antov 26 based in Latvia."

A Russian cargo plane, Ryker knew the specs. "Perfect. You do the pickup in Bulgaria, after that you're on your own. We can do the financial transfer in the Channel Islands, Barclays Offshore."

"Lead time?"

"Three months, minimum. I need the money up front, thirty days prior."

"Agreed," Neils said. He didn't move from his seat. "But there's one more thing."

Ryker raised an eyebrow.

"I have a friend interested in acquiring a single rifle. One very special rifle."

Ryker was surprised at how fast the word had spread. "You were misinformed. I only deal in quantity. Five-hundred piece minimum."

The waiter appeared, but Neils sent him away.

"Let's assume for a moment I am well informed," Neils said. "Might you own something this special?"

Ryker was curious where this would go. "I might."

"Would this rifle come with proper documentation?"

Ryker took a pull on his Bloody Mary. "If I had such a rifle, it would come with excellent documentation." His smile came easier now. "But I can't answer any more questions."

"Just one more, please. Do you know which President's picture came on the ten-thousand dollar bill?"

Ryker hesitated. "I don't get many of those in my line of work."

Neils reached in his jacket breast pocket and removed an envelope. He extracted a single bill and placed it on the table between them. "It's a 1934 Federal Reserve Note, actually."

Ryker leaned forward on his elbows to get a better look. He counted the zeroes and examined the portrait.

"History wasn't my subject."

"It's a trick question. The face on the bill is Salmon Chase, Secretary of the Treasury during the Civil War."

"What's it got to do with us?"

"My friend wants you to have this note for the inconvenience of visiting his office in New York."

Ryker knew a ten-thousand dollar bill was worth considerably more than its face value. "That's a lot of money for an office call. What's he want?"

"A brief conversation is all he asks."

"A conversation." Ryker stared at the zeroes again. "Alright, when?"

"Tomorrow."

"What's the rush?"

Neils shrugged. "It's his way."

Ryker took the bill and put it in a special place in his wallet. "I'll need a name and address. But I can't promise you anything."

"Excellent." Neils put a business card on the table and left without another word.

Ryker finished his drink and stared out at the pouring rain, formulating a new plan. A lot would depend on the business in Arizona, but it just might work.

No.

He would make it work.

Ryker called his driver and told him he'd be late, then motioned to the hovering waiter. Now that things were looking up, dinner seemed like an excellent idea.

***

Sky Harbor's Terminal Three came to life as the first Phoenix business travelers appeared with the dawn. Michael Cole parked his Chevy Tahoe in short-term parking and joined the line snaking inside. He made his way through security and then to American Airline's gate to Dallas, moving slowly as he digested his doubts. A sultry smile from a waiting Kate Marlowe quickened his step. She was seated near the gate with an overnight bag and two cups of coffee.

"Black, or cream and sugar?" she asked.

He dropped his duffel next to her bag. "Black, thank you."

She handed him a paper cup. "You're looking better."

"Yeah. I'm down to one Band-Aid."

She checked his face over. "Still, purple's not your best color."

"I noticed that myself."

She waited. "I wasn't sure you were coming with me."

He removed the coffee lid and inhaled, then took a welcome sip. "I'll admit to second thoughts."

"What made you decide?"

"At first I thought it was the pleasure of your company. Then I decided it must be the TexMex."

Her smile broadened. "In that case, I know the restaurant. Ever been to Dallas?"

Cole shook his head. "I'm curious to see Dealey Plaza, I don't know why I haven't taken the time before now. Bad Juju, I think."

"Your father. Yeah, I know what you mean. After I got divorced, I didn't want to come back to Texas, but it's in my blood."

"What do you do—for work—when you're not making trouble?"

She smiled again. "I'm a legal secretary; I took a leave of absence. The firm was nice enough to give me six weeks' time off."

American Airlines called for seating on their flight, so they got in line and onboard in ten minutes. Cole took the window seat. His expectations grew as the plane taxied for takeoff. They made small talk until cruising altitude, and then Cole quizzed her about the assassination.

"You said it was Carlos Marcello who ordered the hit."

"I think so, I can't be sure," she said.

"Who told him to do it?"

"I think he wanted revenge. The Kennedys had him arrested and deported out of the country." she said. "One pissed-off Mafioso was all you needed."

"So why didn't they arrest the Mafia guys?" he asked.

"Because the Mafia blackmailed J. Edgar Hoover," she said. "They threatened to expose his homosexuality. Somebody had pictures, I'm sure. Hoover used to dress in drag. Picture that."

Cole looked away. "I'd rather not."

"Hoover wouldn't let anyone in the FBI go after them, he said the Mafia didn't exist."

"It could have been a lot of other people," he said.

She shook her head. "I still think it was a Mafia hit. They hated the Kennedys because Bobby had the whole Justice Department after them."

"I know, they felt betrayed," he said. "The Mafia won him Illinois with dead Chicago voters. But they were just the tool for the job."

"So who did it?"

Cole thought. "I think the CIA was involved."

"Too conspiratorial for me," she said.

"So why the government cover-up? Why the insistence it was Lee Harvey Oswald? Why the Warren Report lies?"

"It's just difficult to believe," she said.

"That's what most people think, it's how they got away with it," he said.

"Why CIA?"

"Kennedy was mad at them about forcing the Bay of Pigs fiasco. Said he was gonna bust the CIA into a thousand pieces."

"He took on the big dogs, didn't he?"

"Back then they were like a parallel government, running around the globe, toppling dictators they didn't like."

"Maybe JFK wanted all the power back."

"He fired the top three at the CIA. One of them had a brother who was Mayor of Dallas."

"Just a coincidence," she said.

"You believe in coincidence but not conspiracy?"

"I believe it when I see it."

"Some things you take on faith," he said. I've never seen electrons, but I believe they exist. The CIA had incredible power after WWII."

"What about the Cuban exiles, they were upset over the Bay of Pigs, too."

"They didn't have the resources," he said.

"How about Castro, for the all the CIA plots to kill him?" she asked.

"I don't think he'd risk retaliation. Castro was paranoid we were gonna invade Cuba. The assassination of our President would guarantee it."

"The Russians, then," she said.

"I read the Kremlin was in a panic after it happened. A French reporter was there the next day, he said they were afraid it would go nuclear in retaliation."

She thought. "Kennedy was withdrawing troops from Vietnam. That wasn't popular with the right wingers in the military," she said.

"Nah, too-many people would have known about."

She nodded. "Too hard to keep it quiet."

"Could have been the steel companies. Kennedy forced them to reverse a price increase they needed," he said.

"Not big enough."

A stewardess came by with a tray of orange juice. As Cole took his glass, he spilled a few drops fell on Kate's protruding blouse. He quickly brushed the spill off with his hand. Kate looked down at her breasts, and then over at him.

"Sorry," he said. "I was...I was just cleaning your... blouse."

She held her glass with one hand and smiled at him. "Thank you."

He drank his juice and set the cup on his tray. "Did your father know about your uncle?"

"You mean that he was involved with the Mafia?"

"Or had anything to do with the assassination."

Kate sipped. "If he knew, he never told me. I was too young. I wouldn't have understood, anyway. All I cared about was boys at that age."

"How about now?"

"Males are still on my list. But they're not at the top."

He didn't ask.

"JFK tried to change everything at once," she said. "Maybe it's not so strange he was killed."

"It's not who did it as much as the fact the government covered it up. It makes them look guilty," he said.

"Who is 'the government' anyway? It's just men holding on to their power."

"And men feeding off the process," he said. "Or women."

"But it's men who cause all the trouble." She put her head back.

Cole couldn't argue with that.

CHAPTER FOUR

They were twenty-minutes out of Dallas when the seatbelt light flashed and their 737 began its descent from 37,000 feet. Cole watched out the window as their shadow danced over small ponds, clumps of green trees, and then the rooftops and roads lining the DFW approach.

The landing was smooth. They carried their bags and threaded their way through the terminal to the taxi stand.

"Dealey Plaza," Cole told the driver. He didn't have to give any more information than that, their taxi took off. Cole was impressed by the city's cleanliness as they got close to area.

Delivery trucks and city buses diced for position on the wide, clean streets. Around Dealey Plaza, the city was sprinkled with small parks, while shade trees lined the immaculate sidewalks. Near the convention center, a herd of bronze longhorn steers stood mid trail drive on a grass-covered city block. Rigid cowboys on horseback watched silently over their herd.

Dallas buildings were tall, some newer skyscrapers were 70 stories tall, but the Plaza area was older. Cole commented on the buildings' age and brick construction.

"They were a Roosevelt WPA project," Kate said.

The cab pulled over and let them off at the top of Dealey Plaza.

Cole was struck by two things—how small the plaza was and how many spectators were already there. The whole plaza was only one city block. Thirty to forty people stood on the infamous grassy knoll, pointing and staring off in all directions.

He stopped and looked at the buildings. "It all looks so familiar."

Kate agreed.

The Stemmons Freeway sign was missing and the trees were taller, but everything else looked to Cole as the pictures showed in 1963. One corner of the Plaza held the Texas School Book Depository, its red brick exterior recently sandblasted, the wood window trim freshly-painted dark green. The building's bottom floors were city government offices, while the whole sixth-floor was a museum dedicated to the Kennedy assassination. A special elevator took visitors directly to the Oswald floor.

"Do you want to go up?" she asked.

"Not yet, let's walk around the plaza."

Cole pointed as they walked. "The motorcade was supposed to go straight down Main Street. But that morning they changed the route to pass thru Dealey Plaza."

They strolled down Elm, the street directly in front of the book depository. Cole stepped to the spot where the first shot hit. He turned and looked at the sixth floor Oswald window.

"Look at this." He pointed to show Kate. "The tree is in the view and the angle is too steep. It's a bad location to try a head shot. You've got to swing the rifle sideways to follow the target."

Then he turned and looked at the building directly behind the limousine position. "The DalTex building is a much better choice. You got a clear shot right down the street."

They continued walking down Elm Street, mimicking the limo's movement in 1963. They stopped at the base of the grassy knoll. It was only sixty feet to where Zapruder stood and filmed, and the picket fence at the top of the knoll was even closer.

"Forty people said shots came from behind that fence," Cole said.

Kate pointed at it. "Let's go back there."

They walked up the hill and went behind the wood fence, then stood close to it. Oak trees and pyracantha bushes shielded them from the street view. Cole placed his hand on the top of the pickets.

"It's the perfect height for a man standing here to rest a rifle. It would be hard to miss this shot."

The crowd in the plaza grew larger. Couples strolled around the area, some in their twenties and thirties, a few pushing baby carriages. They all had the same facial expression—somber, reflective, and respectful. Some looked puzzled.

Kate pointed to some writing on the fence; they were comments from people who had visited. One notation stood out.

From this place the world changed.

A tour group arrived with twenty to thirty people. The tour director rattled off names and events Cole knew well; the assassination spectators who had their cameras taken, the man with the black umbrella, the witnesses who later died under mysterious circumstances.

They wandered over to the Book Depository museum entrance and took the elevator to the sixth floor. There were no walls, only large suspended white panels that held photographs and formed walkways through the whole sixth floor. The floor underfoot was the original thick wood planks, now well-worn. Seven large windows filled the wall overlooking Elm Street. More than a hundred people moved through the museum, all wearing the same somber expression.

The photos and exhibits explained life in the early sixties and the JFK mystique to those too young to remember. Hundreds of photos, film clips and artifacts detailed the official assassination story. Abraham Zapruder's 8mm Bell and Howell movie camera was prominently displayed. Cole stopped in front of the exhibit.

"His film was the perfect record," Cole said. "So they only released the frames that supported the Warren Commission Report. Then they locked the film away for eleven years."

They moved next to the corner window where Oswald supposedly shot the President. The Sniper's Nest corner area had a floor-to-ceiling glass wall around it so museum visitors wouldn't disturb the scene. A plaque said police found a 6.5 Mannlicher Carcano rifle there after the shooting, next to some unopened book boxes. The Carcano was an Italian army WWII surplus firearm that Lee Harvey Oswald reputably bought through the mail for $13.50. Cole knew that FBI tests showed the scope was mounted off-center and the rifle was in poor condition.

Kate was curious about the rifle. "Could it have made the shot?" she asked.

Cole scoffed. "Seven expert riflemen tested this shot at a rifle range. They couldn't make it even with a stationary target. And Oswald was no expert, his marksmanship was rated poor by his Marine buddies. He barely qualified as rifleman."

He walked to the next window over and looked down on Elm Street. Trees blocked a clear view of the road.

Kate looked out the window herself. "Doesn't look like the best place to shoot."

Cole agreed. They moved on. Videos of black and white television clips ran in the next exhibit. The videos showed news announcers recounting the first few moments after the shots were fired, and finally a young Walter Cronkite fighting back tears as he gave the terrible news of Kennedy's death to the nation.

On their way out, Cole and Kate walked by a glass case standing all alone. It held fine China plates, crystal glassware and the silver cutlery originally set at the Dallas Trade Center, JFK's final scheduled stop in Dallas. The image was a solitary place setting, waiting for a luncheon guest that never came. Kate frowned as they exited the museum.

"I can't help feeling somehow guilty for what happened," she said.

Cole nodded. "I think the whole nation felt disgusted."

Out front entrepreneurs had booths setup to sell memorabilia. They stopped at a vendor selling reprints of Dallas newspapers from the assassination week. The young man wore an orange tee shirt with a University of Texas logo.

They gave him a twenty for two papers. "Are you an assassination buff?" Cole asked.

"Nah. My dad follows it, I'm just after beer money."

"Is your dad local?" Kate asked.

"Dallas. All his life."

"Who's he think killed Kennedy?"

"Probably the only ones not involved were Castro and the KGB. Anyone could have fired the shots. But he thinks LBJ was the one behind it."

"Why LBJ?"

"Johnson hated the Kennedys. Pardon my saying, but Johnson said they treated him like he had shit on his boots."

Kate laughed. "Fighting words from a Texan."

"He knew all the Texas oilmen, the shady Texas crooks, the Mafia guys, and the Dallas police. He even lived on the same street as J Edgar Hoover."

"That doesn't mean he did it," Cole said.

The vendor shrugged. "No, but there's one thing. Johnson had that limo rebuilt two days after the assassination. Why would you do that unless you wanted to hide evidence?"

"What evidence could be in the car?" Kate asked.

"Gunshot holes. My dad has an old photo of the limo dashboard taken that day. It shows a bullet hole at the base of the windshield. No way could that shot come from the Oswald window. It had to come from another building, something behind the car."

They thanked him and moved on to the corner where a hotdog vendor was doing a brisk business.

"Do you want to get something?" Kate asked

"Yeah." Cole rubbed his temples. "Let's get a drink."

CHAPTER FIVE

Mark Sidney was on the lowest rung of the employee ladder at the Missouri Bureau of Alcohol, Tobacco and Firearms and he was damn glad to be there. Saddled with a hundred-thousand-dollar loan after five years at Texas A&M obtaining his economics degree, Sidney gladly took a simple tech position in the Kansas City ATF Field Office. He had the latest computer hardware, his own cubicle and a flexible work schedule.

Sidney came in early lugging a Starbucks Venti Latte so he didn't have to start the day with the cheap government brew. He checked his email first—an afternoon department meeting, the office vacation schedule—but nothing from Jodie. He thought about calling his girl, but decided it could wait until lunch. He wanted to get to work and keep his boss happy.

As far as he was concerned, they were paying him a ridiculous amount of money to surf the web, something he did anyway. His job was lurking online at the many web firearm forums and chat rooms. Thomas, his boss, said the best way to know what was really going on out there was to listen to the chatter. What are they buying? What are they making in their home workshops? Who's skirting the rules?

If he saw a post on how to build your own silencer—the ATF will ask the forum boss to remove the post. If someone tries to sell a Class III firearm without the paperwork—then they'll get a friendly visit from a Special Agent.

Sidney turned on his monitor and went to the AR15 forum first. He checked the For Sale section, and then went on to the political stuff. The usual posters had been there late the night before, spewing the same old Second Amendment fears after too-much whiskey. They were harmless.

But then he saw it again. Three new posts on it this time. He flicked over to National Firearm forum. Four new posts.

Sidney took his latte with him and went to see Assistant Special Agent Aaron Thomas in his front office. He knocked twice on the open metal door.

"Got a second, boss?"

Thomas waved him in and eyed the Starbucks paper cup. "You got a problem with our coffee here, Mister Sidney?"

"No, sir. I'm all in favor of developing new biofuels. I think it's a wonderful experiment."

Thomas' smile was thin. "What's up?"

"I'm seeing a lot of posts on the Kennedy assassination, it started a week ago."

"So?"

"The word on the street is the Kennedy rifle has surfaced."

"The Carcano? It's buried in the National Archives."

"No. They say the real rifle; the one that actually killed JFK is going to be auctioned on the fiftieth anniversary. November twenty-second."

Thomas tapped his pencil on the desktop. "Go on."

"No one thinks the 6.5 Mannlicher Carcano hit the President, or was even used. The pictures from that day show two different rifles. They think the Carcano was a plant."

"So what's the real rifle supposed to be?"

"They don't talk about the type of gun—or the caliber. They just say the actual rifle from the grassy knoll shot."

"Sounds like internet crap to me."

"Maybe. But that's what you pay me to find."

Thomas thought a minute, then asked. "Is this any forum in particular?"

"National Firearms, AR15, couple others."

"Probably just conspiracy nuts putting garbage out. These guys have too-much time on their hands. I wouldn't put any stock in it."

"I suppose." Sidney didn't move from the doorway, he wasn't convinced. "But this is what bothers me. The Wall Street guys know the stock market moves ahead of the event, that prices rise or fall before the news. Like before the unemployment numbers come out, or a Fed policy change."

"Thanks, I read the Wall Street Journal."

"They say that all information is in the market, all of the time."

"Is that what they taught you in college, mister econ major?"

"The point is you can't keep anything secret. Everything is out there. People talk. There's got to be something to the rumor, it's coming from too-many different sources."

Thomas rocked back in his chair. "How much was that?" He pointed at Sidney's paper coffee cup.

"The Starbucks? Four bucks. Why?"

"Lemme give you my economics lesson, Sidney. That Starbucks is costing you a lot more than four dollars. Figure what you'll save if you pay that towards your school loan. Say it takes you twenty years to pay it off your debt.

47

You're probably holding a twenty dollar cup of coffee there."

"Could be. But in twenty years a latte will cost twenty dollars. So what should I do about this?"

Thomas picked up a file from his desk and flipped it open. "If I were you, I'd save your money and drink the government slop. Go back to work and don't worry about John Kennedy or his rifle. That's ancient history."

When Sidney was gone, Assistant Special Agent Thomas closed the file and stared out in space. Then he picked up the phone and called the ATF Deputy Director in Washington, DC.

***

Kate and Cole walked from Dealey Plaza to a TexMex restaurant just winding down from the lunch rush. They took a booth in the back.

A waiter appeared as they were considering drinks.

"Modelo," he said.

"Margarita," she said.

She turned to Cole. "That was moving, seeing the museum. And the displays were…"

Kate talked on about the sixth floor but he didn't hear. He was thinking about her face. He thought she was attractive, but for the first time he realized Hollywood would not. She had some flaw—a millimeter or two off, a canted angle, some feature mismatch he couldn't identify—but the sum total worked for him. Worked well.

She stopped talking, and he realized she'd asked him a question.

"I'm sorry?" he asked.

"I said, did we learn anything today?"

He thought back. "It was good to see the Plaza in person instead of photographs. I liked seeing the view from the sniper window. And I was surprised to see so many people in the museum."

When the drinks arrived, Cole held up his beer and proposed a toast. "To lone assassins."

"Everywhere." She took a sip, then another.

He set his drink next to hers. "Your father. What'd he do in Texas?"

"He was a deep-water driller—oil rigs in the Gulf of Mexico. He wasn't home much, and one time he didn't come home at all. Killed when a rig blew, he was only forty-seven."

"How old were you?"

"Thirteen. My parents were divorced and my mom had moved away. My uncle took care of me best he could, but I was a handful. Eventually I went away to college. When I finally graduated, I worked in a law firm until I got married."

"How old was your uncle when he died?"

"Seventy-four. He was closer to me than I was to him, but I owe him a lot."

"Why'd he tell you about Kennedy?"

"He thought he was going to die. He wasn't a religious man, but he wanted to make his peace with the world. If that's possible." She looked down. "It's a horrible thing they did."

Cole didn't add to that.

Kate took a drink. "What about your dad?" she asked him.

"After he was shot, he spent a lot of time recuperating." Cole finished his beer. "He started to talk about it with the authorities. Then weird stuff happened, he said. Men showed up late at night at his door, warning him to keep quiet."

"Did he?"

"For a while. Then he tried to get his story in front of the Warren Commission. He got death threats, finally somebody shot out his apartment windows. He moved to Phoenix two days later."

The waiter returned for their requests. Kate ordered Shrimp Fajitas; he got the Chile con Carne, something he didn't normally find in Phoenix.

"Were you born in Arizona?" Kate asked.

"To my dad's second wife, 1975. Grew up in Phoenix, did some time in the service—first Gulf War—then with the Phoenix Police."

"And now you're an expert."

"Only about firearms." He smiled at her. "Never figured out women."

"You didn't marry?"

"Divorced," he said.

"Why didn't you remarry?"

"Never met the right woman."

She played with her glass. "Maybe you did, but you didn't know it."

"That sounds like the sober voice of experience."

She combed her hair back with one hand. "Men are hard to figure," she said.

Cole shook his head. "Not me, I'm a simple guy. I think it's women who are complicated."

"We're easier to understand than you think."

"Someday you'll have to tell me the secret."

"That's against girl rules."

"You have rules?" he asked. "That's cheating."

"Spoken by a specie member whose only concern is spreading their DNA."

"A biological necessity beyond our control. At least males are honest about it."

"No they aren't."

"What about women? They're not sneaky?"

"Women deceive men to keep them around to raise their offspring," she said.

"Is that one of the rules or just an excuse?"

"Sorry," she said. "We're sworn to secrecy. Never let men know the truth."

"Because we'd lose interest?"

She smiled sweetly. "Because you can't handle the truth."

Kate locked eyes with him as she pressed her thigh against his. He felt a quickening of heart and a stirring of suppressed passion. She moved her hand to his leg and softly rested it there. Then...

"Who had the chili?" It was the waiter with two plates.

Kate moved back and picked up her napkin.

They ate in silence a while, then Cole spoke. "What'd your uncle expect you to do about all this?"

She paused. "Just prove he was part of a conspiracy. Go get the rifle, he said. The rifle will help get the attention you need. More people will talk once it surfaces."

"What was his name?"

"Billy Marlowe."

"He told you all this on his deathbed?" Cole asked.

"No, it was about three months before he died. He asked me to wait until he passed. It's not that he was afraid of being arrested, just harassed with media questions."

"What about the shooter, what happened to him?"

"He died in the late sixties, killed by someone during a bank robbery. Never went to jail, for murder or anything else."

"How'd your uncle end up with the rifle in the first place? I'd have thought it'd be at the bottom of some lake," he asked.

"That was their screwup. He was supposed to get rid of it, but he hung on to it in case he needed a bargaining chip."

"I'm surprised they let him take it."

She leaned forward. "He was the driver. It was his job to transport the rifle to and from Dealey Plaza. They cut compartments in the doors and trunk and hid their guns behind panels. He had one of those big Oldsmobiles, he said, a '60 or '61. Not sure.

"The plan was for my uncle and the shooter to drive to Arizona and lay-low for six weeks. Somewhere around Gallup they had engine trouble, so my uncle stayed with the car and the guns and the shooter took a bus to Tucson to hide-out. The car was done in a couple days so my uncle drove to a Tucson motel to meet him."

"So the gun's been there all this time?"

"Hopefully," she said.

"What do you mean, hopefully? You don't know?"

"No. At least I'm not sure."

"Are you even sure it's there?" he asked.

"Well, no. Not without looking."

"No?" Cole dropped his fork. "What the hell does that mean?"

"I know where my uncle left it in 1963, I'm pretty sure it's still there."

Cole sighed. He'd thought this was a sure thing, now it looked more like a treasure hunt. "Kate. You're killing me. Where do we find it?"

"It's hidden at a ranch."

"In Arizona?"

"Southern Arizona," she said.

"That's a pretty big area."

"It's all I can tell you now, be patient."

"I've been patient," he said.

"Have some trust, then."

"There's plenty of trust here. But it's all on my end."

"I trust you, but it's important to wait."

Cole wondered if he had a choice at all.

Kate finished her plate. "Come with me to find it. When's the last time you changed history?"

Cole sighed. "Don't worry, I'm coming. What's the plan?"

"I'm going home to Houston for a couple days, and then I'll come see you in Phoenix." She looked at him closely, her eyes soft in the light. "Are you spending the night in Dallas?"

"I should get back to Phoenix."

She hesitated. "I know a good breakfast spot."

"That sounds...interesting."

She toyed with her hair. "Only interesting?"

He was tempted. But it was a bad idea and he knew it. "It might complicate things."

"It might," she said. "It probably would."

"You like complicated?"

"I'm trying to show you some trust."

Cole placed his hand on hers. "I appreciate that. But remember, I'm a simple kinda guy."

"You don't seem like a simple guy to me."

He smiled. "Is that good or bad?"

"I'm trying to decide. It's intriguing, at least."

"What do your girl rules tell you?"

"To be careful."

"That's all I'm doing."

They said nothing for a moment, lost in thought.

Finally Cole spoke. "I better take the late afternoon flight home. I think I can make that. I've got a deposition scheduled tomorrow at a Phoenix lawyer's office."

"Deposition? You being sued?"

"No, it's one of the services I provide. Helps pay the rent."

"Of course," she said.

They sat a minute.

Finally Cole asked. "Ready to go?"

Kate put both palms on the table. "I'll meet you in Phoenix in two days. We'll drive down south and find the real Kennedy rifle."

"Meet me in Scottsdale," he said. "Not Phoenix."

"Phoenix, Scottsdale, what's the difference?"

"Scottsdale." Cole dropped some cash on the table. "Less crime, more silicone."

CHAPTER SIX

James William Moffet credited his success on Wall Street to a mathematics degree from M.I.T. and his government years with the N.S.A. It turned out the math needed for code-cracking worked even better in the stock market. Moffet's best year was plus 61 percent. It was also the worst year in a decade for the Dow Jones.

Moffet was a quant. He built his trading algorithms using *invariants*, the mathematics used to distinguish among curved spaces—the kind of distortions of ordinary space that exist according to Einstein's General Theory of Relativity. James Moffet liked to say it was easier to predict the course of a comet than the future price of the S&P 500. He could do both with accuracy, but his option trading made him a billionaire.

His concern at the moment was a trade of a different kind, one that fed his expensive hobby collecting rare historical artifacts. He already owned an original Gutenberg Bible, one of two stolen Dead Sea Scrolls, and a very unique firearm from the nineteenth century. He was about to show that firearm to his visitor, Robert Ryker, a man who dealt in insecurity, not securities.

Moffet opened the safe in his minimalist office on the fifty-fifth floor of the MetLife building, then handed the firearm to his guest. Ryker examined the weapon closely.

It was a crude but deadly pistol; approximately 6 inches long, with a checkered black walnut stock, S-shaped trigger guard, and a grooved hammer thumb piece. The brown barrel was chemically-stained wrought iron with silver detailing.

"German silver inlay," Moffet pointed out.

"Caliber?"

"Seven groove, two and a half-inch barrel with .41 caliber."

Ryker hefted it in his hand. "Light. Must be only eight, ten ounces." He extended the pocket pistol to the firing position. "But good balance."

Moffet grew animated, happy to show his artifact to an appreciative enthusiast. "They were usually sold in pairs, along with the bullet mold for both pistols. Unfortunately, neither its twin nor the molds were available."

Ryker examined the markings on the barrel. "Derringer Philadela."

"From his Philadelphia factory. It was Henry Derringer's trademark. They all had it."

"No serial numbers?"

"He didn't use them. In 1864 they didn't sell that many."

Ryker frowned. "Then how can you be sure?"

"There were authenticating photos taken of the pistol in its display at the Ford Theater Museum. The tooling marks and wood grain are clear and unique, and an exact match to the pistol in your hand. I have the photographs, of course. They're from the National Park Service, taken during the Depression."

"Fascinating," Ryker said.

"Do you see the small crack in the wood grip?"

He turned it over to examine the faint flaw. "Yes."

"That's where John Wilkes Booth dropped it when he jumped from Lincoln's box to the stage."

Ryker placed the pistol carefully on the desk. "When was it acquired?

"During a 1969 robbery at the Ford Theater display." Moffet chuckled at the thought. "Crude security at best. They swapped an identical-appearing derringer for the Booth derringer. It was ten years before it was discovered, then authorities covered it up."

"Typical bureaucrats," Ryker said. "What do you think its worth? One million? Two million?"

"Please. It's not about the money. This is a piece of history that changed our nation. I'm just the caretaker."

Ryker folded his arms. "And you know I have a similar piece."

"The Kennedy sniper rifle."

"I assume you're interested."

"Very. The rumor is you're planning an auction."

"It's true. I see now why you have such interest in our rifle. To own both the Lincoln and the Kennedy assassination firearms, that would be an unbelievable collection."

"Of course. That's what I want to talk about," Moffett said.

"I assure you, the authentication is very reliable. You won't be disappointed."

"I'm not concerned about that, but I will do my own checking, of course."

"Then—what is it?" Ryker asked. "The auction participants?"

"No. I'm not interested in bidding at your auction. I want to buy the Kennedy rifle outright."

Ryker looked surprised. "Surely you see my position. An auction on the fiftieth anniversary would be a very special event."

"No doubt it would get you top dollar. But I'm willing to pay you that amount right now."

"Mister Moffet—"

"Call me James. What figure did you have in mind?"

"I'm sorry. I didn't come here prepared to sell. I'll need to think about it."

Moffet walked to the window overlooking Central Park and gazed on the spring green below. Finally he turned. "That's not true. I'm sure you know exactly what you'll take. You've thought about it a lot."

Ryker said nothing.

"Give me your price, Mister Ryker, or this meeting is over."

Moments passed. "I believe it will approach five million dollars."

If the figure shocked Moffet he didn't show it. "Very well. I will give you six million to assure you are getting the best price."

"I don't believe—"

Moffet held up his hand. "I can go six-five, but don't ask for more. Do you agree or not?"

"Agreed."

"Excellent. When can you deliver? I can wire transfer as soon as I see the piece."

Ryker squirmed visibly in his chair. "We're moving a little too fast, I'm afraid. Delivery is a problem right now. I will need a few weeks."

"Mister Ryker. Please don't tell me you're wasting my time. Do you have the rifle that killed Kennedy or don't you?"

"I assure you, I can deliver in two weeks. Right now there are some loose ends."

"Very well." Moffet placed the John Wilkes Booth derringer back in its wood case and moved it to the safe. "We'll talk again when you're prepared." Moffet stared coldly. "I'm assuming you're a man of your word. Don't disappoint me."

***

Michael Cole sat in the conference room of Baxter & Welsley's Phoenix Law Offices with a foot-high stack of files, a court stenographer, and Phoenix attorney Charles E. Baxter. During the deposition, Cole's job was to prove his expertise. Baxter hoped to prove otherwise.

Baxter did the questioning. "Would you state your name, please?"

"Michael Cole. C-o-l-e."

"I received and read your resume. Is this an updated version?"

"It is."

"I have a few questions about it. You were with the Phoenix Police Department?"

"Yes, as an armorer."

"Explain that, please."

"I performed firearm maintenance for the department, acquisition advice and ballistic research."

"Your firm now, Ballistic FX, is that a testing company?"

"We do some freelance ballistic development, lectures, and courtroom testimony."

"What are the terms of your engagement, Mister Cole?"

"For deposition and testimony, my fee is $300 an hour. For investigation and research, it's $100 an hour."

"Then your personal expertise is in the field of ballistics?"

"It is."

"Would that include wound ballistics?"

"It would."

"But you're not a medical doctor?"

"No."

"Where did you acquire your knowledge of wound ballistics?"

"Mostly from Fackler and Matunas' work. Also the International Wound Ballistic Symposiums, and the Relative Incapacitation Index studies."

"What is that last one?"

"RCI looks at the effect of different caliber bullets on various areas of the body. It was created to assist law-enforcement agencies in their choice of weapons."

"So you have a pretty good understanding of which calibers, which firearms are most deadly."

"I do," Cole said.

"Would you consider the .38 special a deadly weapon?"

"It's a relatively small, low-velocity round, but it would be deadly at close range—with a hit in the body's vital zone."

"Do you consider the leg a vital zone?"

"No, sir."

"In your studies of wound ballistics, did you find examples of .38 caliber shootings resulting in death?"

"Many."

"How many deaths did you find from leg wounds?"

"I can't recall any."

"None. Did you receive the x-rays of Officer Johnson's leg wound?"

"I did."

The defendant—Doctor William Kyle—was being sued for malpractice in the death of a police officer who developed a lethal case of gas gangrene after being shot with a .38 caliber revolver. The plaintiff—the officer's family—claimed the doctor's surgery was too little and too late. Cole was hired by the doctor and the hospital.

"Did you see anything unusual, anything deadly about this wound to his leg?"

"I did not."

"Did you read the hospital report of the surgery?"

"Yes."

"Then you must have read the surgical exploration of the wound did not take place until 40 hours after he was shot. In your expert opinion, Mister Cole, was that unusual?"

Cole knew where the lawyer was going with this. "No, and that's the problem."

The plaintiff attorney looked up quickly. "Are you saying the physician's negligence resulted in the death of Officer Johnson?"

"No. I'm not a physician, I can't comment on standard of care, only on the behavior of bullets. But I can tell you what happens to tissue with a bullet wound.

"When a bullet penetrates human flesh, the initial tissue-crush is called the permanent cavity. The surrounding tissue displacement from kinetic-energy transfer is called the temporary cavity. This temporary cavity is much larger when the projectile is a high-velocity round. Surgeons tend to remove this tissue, but not tissue surrounding a low-velocity strike."

"So was the treatment administered by Doctor Kyle 'wrong' in your opinion?"

"I'm saying it was standard treatment. Doctor Kyle followed current medical thinking, but it's my opinion that thinking is flawed. "

Cole settled back in his chair. "In this instance the results were tragic, but Doctor Kyle's actions were common, medically-accepted procedure."

CHAPTER SEVEN

Brian Ross walked briskly to the east end of Washington's National Mall and entered the National Gallery of Art. He scanned the bottom floor to get the lay of the land, more out of habit than necessity. The prominent exhibit that month was a collection of works by Winslow Homer, a painter some critics considered America's greatest artist. Ross paused in front of a Homer painting entitled 'Gulf Stream', featuring a lone sailor lying on the deck of a small, dismasted boat surrounded by a ring of predatory sharks.

It seemed fitting.

Brian Ross reported directly to the Director of Alcohol, Tobacco and Firearms. He did housecleaning, obfuscation and CYA for the Director, and had been hustling to keep up in recent days. It was the reason for the day's meeting with a similar compatriot working for the U.S. Justice Department.

Ross proceeded to the upper level. He entered the Gallery's in-house Terrace Café and took a small table overlooking the National Mall. Two cobalt-blue place settings graced the fresh, white linen tablecloth. It was too early for dinner and too late for lunch, as evidenced by the lack of patrons. He ordered an ice tea with lemon and waited. Half a glass later he was joined by an impeccably dressed gentleman, mid-fifties, dark blue suit and closely-cropped grey hair.

"Coffee, please." Blue Suit smiled at the waiter but not Brian Ross. "Alright. What's up with this Kennedy thing?" he asked.

Ross stirred his tea, choosing his words carefully. "I thought Justice should be in the loop. I don't think it's anything we can't keep a lid on, but you should know. It's an election year. Why feed the jackals?"

Blue suit nodded. "The Tea Party would go nuts, talk radio would have a field day. Not to mention the Anti-Wall Street crowd. The administration can't afford an old Kennedy conspiracy to surface right now."

"What should we do?" Ross asked.

"First things first. Are you sure about this?"

"The story's come all the way up the ladder, we've heard it from every district, even overseas. We know something about this Robert Ryker. Normally his arms dealings are offshore. He has accounts in the Channel Islands, but we can't access them."

"I know, Justice is looking into Ryker. Could he have this rifle?"

Ross shrugged. "Anyone can claim they have the rifle that killed Kennedy. That's like saying you've got George Washington's cherry-tree hatchet."

"He's setting up an auction with major players. Ryker's got something to sell." Blue Suit took a sip of his coffee. "I don't think it's bullshit."

"We have our doubts."

"That's nice, but they don't pay ATF to analyze. Tell me what kind of rifle we're looking for."

Ross let the insult go. "I can tell you what our gun guys are saying. They think the weapon used on the knoll was a Remington Fireball."

"Never heard of it."

"It's a single-shot target pistol. Actually, more like a short-barrel rifle with a pistol grip. Barrel's only eleven inches. The first models came out in 1963, so that works."

"What caliber is it?"

"It's a .221, something like a short .556 NATO round. But the first year it was chambered for the .222, which has more powder. Remember the reports of smoke from the Grassy Knoll?"

"Not up on that."

"The .222 had too-much powder for the short barrel, it shot smoke and flame out the muzzle. That's another reason it could have been used that day. Plus it was deadly accurate, and a perfect size for a sniper on the knoll to conceal."

"I've seen the autopsy photos, and the Zapruder film. Kennedy was shot in the throat first."

"Right. They said the neck wound was a hospital tracheotomy, but the small wound size looked more like a .22 caliber bullet hole, not a trache."

"Can you get me a picture of this Fireball?"

"I'll email you one, but the wood stocks varied."

Blue Suit finished writing some notes. "Looks like I got what I need, then."

"So what's next?"

"I think Justice should take it from here."

"Hold on," Ross said. "ATF is better able to follow up on this, it's our area."

"Sorry. You guys screw-up too much. Besides, your reputation needs some healing after that Mexico gun-running fiasco."

Ross bristled. "I heard that program came directly from you guys."

"Doesn't matter. It's ATF who stepped on their dick."

Ross didn't want to let that one go. "The House Select Committee recommended the Justice Department investigate the conspiracy. You just now getting around to it? Maybe a little fiftieth-anniversary surprise?"

"Never gonna happen. Any investigation died with Kennedy."

"What do you know about it?"

"Enough, but not everything."

"So who did it?"

"Who killed Kennedy? That's the wrong question."

Ross considered that. "Humor me."

"I don't know who pulled the trigger and I don't care. But ask yourself, who could cover-up something this big? Who got everybody in line, from Earl Warren to J. Edgar to the Dallas Police? That's the question."

"The CIA."

"Partly. Half the cover-up came from compromised agencies, like the CIA. They didn't want to admit they screwed up."

"What about the FBI?"

"The mob controlled Hoover; he wouldn't admit the Mafia even existed. He certainly wouldn't admit he blew the chance to stop Oswald."

"So you're saying—"

"I'm saying nothing. My concern is getting this rifle—if there is one—before it does any damage to the administration. That's what they pay me for. Prevention, not damage control. I need to be in front of this."

"What about Ryker?"

"We've been listening in on his phone. What do you know about Arizona?"

Ross hesitated a split second, suddenly not interested in helping. "Arizona? Nothing, why?"

"Ryker's got a couple guys in working Phoenix, and they don't sound like Boy Scouts. We're gonna send a man down there."

"We have men in Phoenix."

"You guys are done." Blue Suit stood up. "Send me everything else you have and stay out of our way."

He walked out.

When the Justice agent was gone, Ross sat a while considering his next move. He decided to do nothing. It was better this way. If it blew-up in someone's face, better it be the Justice Department.

Ross gazed out at the mall. Tourists strolled and locals scurried, oblivious to the Washington power struggles all around them. It was a waste of time and resources. Administrations wasted their first-term planning and conniving for a second.

He finished his tea and motioned for the check. On his way out of the gallery, he glanced once more at Homer's 'Gulf Stream' painting.

The sharks were still circling.

CHAPTER EIGHT

Michael Cole's three-bedroom house was in North Phoenix, close to the town of Carefree and far from strip malls and traffic. He bought the home in a short sale after the housing bust when rates were reasonable and he had a little cash.

He'd furnished it with verde leather couches, then some equipale chairs and wormwood tables he'd dragged back from Mexico. The imports went well with his Mexican-tile floors, and he liked the worn, lived-in feeling they encouraged. They didn't clash with his level of cleaning, either.

The house came with a lap pool, so he had the swimming benefits a pool provided and the maintenance curse it demanded.

The pristine water still held the mild winter's chill, but Cole needed to clear his head. He pulled on a thin O'Neil spring wetsuit and dove in. A dozen laps later he felt refreshed and ready to formulate a plan. He stretched out on a pool lounge chair and let the warm April sun dry his skin. His injuries were healing, the bandages were gone. All that was left was a multi-color bruise.

Cole prepared himself for the next phase of the rifle search, whatever that may be. He was mildly optimistic and a bit intrigued by Kate Marlowe.

He was not without some doubts, however, so he'd pulled strings with old friends at the Phoenix police department to check into Kate's background. She came out clean. Her ex-husband was a rich Houston tax attorney and her father had indeed been an offshore oil worker. Marlowe was her maiden name, but it provided no clues to her mysterious uncle's background. Cole thought an alias was probably used for most of the criminal's career.

As far as finding the rifle that killed Kennedy, he was only hopeful and still not convinced. Fifty years seemed too long. In his experience, not much remained the same after five decades. Memories, maybe. Painful memories for sure.

From his chair at poolside, Cole picked up the newspaper reprints he bought in Dealey Plaza from the vendor. The first was *The Dallas Times Herald*, November 22nd Final Edition.

PRESIDENT DEAD
CONNALLY SHOT

He skimmed the articles with their eyewitness reports. One woman said she heard six shots. A man said Kennedy was hit from the front or side. The rifle used in the assassination was reported to be a .30 caliber. Another woman only heard three shots.

Cole picked up the other paper, *The Evening Star*, Extra Edition, also from November 22nd.

SNIPER KILLS KENNEDY
JOHNSON IS PRESIDENT

The articles were more of the same—stunned crowds, frantic searches, shocked and weeping spectators. No one knew how bad it was going to get after Jack Ruby killed Oswald.

They discovered the Washington DC phone system went down right after the assassination. Then it was learned every member of the President's cabinet was out of the country. Over the next few years, witnesses started dying, some on the day before they were set to testify.

Cole set the papers aside. It was understandable people grew reluctant to talk about the assassination. But now, after fifty years, who would still care?

He was still thinking about it when he heard his phone ring. He rolled off the lounger and went inside to answer.

"It's Kate," the voice said. "I'm in town at the Gateway."

"Are you ready to travel?" he asked.

"I am. I've got a week's worth of underwear and a secret treasure map. Can you top that?"

He grinned at the mental picture. "I doubt if I can improve on that combination. But I'll bring a GPS and my .45."

"Bring a road map, too. Can you pick me up?"

They made plans for when and where. Cole showered, dressed, and packed a bag, then gave the house a once over, not knowing when he'd be back.

His Tahoe was already backed in the garage. He popped the trunk and threw a clothes bag inside along with some hand tools. His gas tank was full, so the only thing left to load was weapons.

Cole placed a nylon range bag on the garage workbench and unzipped the top. He put in four loaded HK magazines and two boxes of 45ACP ammunition. He hesitated, then added some field binoculars, a cleaning kit and a handful of cotton rags.

He returned to the house and went to his wall safe. He spun the combination and removed some bills, then stuck a handful of hundreds in his wallet. He checked the HK chamber for a loaded round then placed it back on his hip, cocked and locked. He took one last look around. It was time to go.

He pulled out of the driveway and idled through his neighborhood. A quarter of the subdivision houses sat empty, waiting for a change in the economy to bring buyers or a rental occupant. He waved to a neighbor, then sped up on a deserted stretch of road.

Cole drove north toward the Scottsdale resort section, growing in optimism and elevating in mood. Maybe it was the prospect of seeing Kate. Maybe it was the prospect of finally finding some hard proof in the assassination.

Early afternoon traffic was light and Kate's hotel was close to the freeway, so he made good time getting to the Gateway. He called her cell from the parking lot and in a few minutes she appeared with a small suitcase in hand.

She looked like she understood Southern Arizona. Kate was wearing a white cotton blouse, skin-tight Levis and hiking boots. She grinned.

Her smile was growing on him. He got out and opened the trunk for her bag, still affixed with a PHX flight tag.

"You hungry?" he asked.

"I ate lunch in the restaurant, not bad, not good."

"We can get something better for dinner."

When they hit the freeway, Cole set the cruise control at five over the limit. "Where are we going?" he asked. "Or is that a secret?"

"Tucson, for starters." She looked at the dash. "Where's your GPS?"

"It's in the trunk."

"Why not plug it in?" she asked.

"I know where Tucson is."

"Sure, but the GPS tells you how far and where to turn."

"Maybe I want to take a different route," he said. "That voice is only gonna nag me to correct my route."

"It's comforting."

"It's annoying. It's like continually asking directions and having someone tell you how to get there. Why do I need a woman's voice nagging me while I drive?"

"Especially when you have me," she said.

"Exactly."

"How far is it?"

"Two, maybe two and a half hours." He handed her a road map. She unfolded it and studied the southern Arizona roads.

Finally she put it down. "If we had the GPS—"

"We don't need that much information."

"Why? Are you one of those pre-digital kinda guys? Can't program your alarm clock?"

"I get up with the sun. Does that make me a Neanderthal?"

"Technically, yes," she said.

"Neanderthal man had a bigger brain and a stronger body."

"Yeah, but he didn't invent anything as good as a global positioning."

"We're not in a hurry, are we? It's been nearly fifty years, we can kill a little time."

"It's just…" She looked out the window.

"Just what?"

"This search may be a little bit more difficult than I led you to believe."

"Kate—"

"Now don't be mad. We only have to work harder."

"Lemme guess. You don't actually know where the rifle is."

She reached in her purse and pulled out a large manila envelope. "It's all in here—where the gun is—but it isn't clear. Perfectly clear, anyway."

Cole sighed. "Is there any more bad news you're sitting on? Let's get it all out."

"That's it, I swear."

Cole looked over at the envelope in her hand. "What've you got there?"

She opened it and removed a folded yellowed newspaper wrapped in plastic. "It's a Tucson Daily Star from three days after the assassination, November 26th, 1963. My uncle gave it to me, it's been in a safe deposit box or under his mattress all this time."

"You said the rifle was at a ranch."

She nodded. "He said it's in the wall of one of the cabins, the one they were hiding out at."

"And the ranch is still there?"

"It better be, or we're gonna feel pretty stupid."

He was familiar with southern Arizona. "There's a good chance it's still there. Most of the state is the same now as it was in the sixties, a lot of it isn't even airconditioned, much less repainted in the last two decades."

"I'm sure this place won't be."

"Where is it?" Cole asked.

She held up the newspaper and read. "Near Willcox—you know where that is?"

"East of Tucson." He handed her an older road map. "Then where?"

"He told me the ranch is north of Willcox, just follow the directions on the paper. She read the scribbling in the margins. "Willcox, 45 miles north 12 east. Fort Grant, room wall." She looked at him and smiled triumphantly.

He kept his eyes on the road. "That's it?"

"You need more?"

"What's 12 east mean?"

"Twelve miles east," she said.

"East of what?"

"East of Fort Grant something."

"Maybe. Or maybe it means twelve *feet* east to the wall. Or maybe an east wall twelve feet long," he said.

"Gad, you are such a pessimist. It's clearly 45 miles north and 12 miles east."

"Forty-five miles north of what?"

"The town of Willcox," she said.

"On the road or as the crow flies?"

"Is this why you got divorced?"

"Because I ask questions?" he asked.

"Your glass is always half empty."

"That's all you got?"

"You need more mouth than that?" she asked.

"I mean, do you have any more directions? What about Fort Grant?"

"I think it means Fort Grant Road, it runs through that area. So I googled the satellite view and found two possible ranches."

"Great, one of them is probably used for drug running."

"Half-empty," she said.

He ignored her. "That area is full of traffickers, the Sinaloa Cartel is all over the place bringing product north."

"You've got a big gun, don't you, tough guy?"

"I didn't bring enough firepower for Mexican drug cartels. Best to avoid them."

"You're teasing me, aren't you?" she asked.

"Not entirely. You can get unlucky down there. I heard of guys getting killed for their pickup truck."

"Don't worry." She smiled sweetly. "I'm feeling lucky these days."

Cole considered the implications. "So we go to Willcox and try to find this ranch. Did he tell you anything about who owned it? A name, perhaps?"

"It was a hideout for mob guys, not a bed and breakfast."

"What'd they raise on this ranch? It might help us find it."

"Cattle, I would think," she said.

"They also dug out copper and gold in that part of the state."

"That would make it a mine, wouldn't it? We're looking for a ranch. Cattle, you know, like moo-cows?"

"Is that why *you* got divorced? That mouth?"

She looked out the window at the blur of desert green. "My husband was sleeping with his secretary. Among others."

"Sorry."

"You should be, men are pigs. How much further? Check the GPS—oh that's right."

He thought. "I'd guess an hour or so. Why?"

"I have to pee."

"Can you go on the side of the road?"

She looked at him in horror.

"Alright, alright. There's a rest stop coming up soon."

He pulled off the highway three-miles later and Kate got out with her purse.

"Be right back," she said.

Cole rolled down the window and let the weather in. Soon it would be triple digits and every door and window would be shut for half the year. It was like living in an airconditioned can, he thought. Get it now while you can.

He picked up Kate's old Tucson paper and examined the writing from so long ago. The yellow paper was brittle but her uncle's ink was still legible. He kept the paper up in front of his face, but moved his rear-view mirror sideways and looked at a maroon Camaro parked down the line. The two men in the front seat hadn't moved since they pulled in the rest stop behind them. He tried to get a look at them, but couldn't make out any detail.

Kate emerged from the bathroom and returned to the car.

"Thanks, I feel much better now," she said.

Cole backed the Tahoe into the exit lane and adjusted his mirror, then followed a semi truck moving slowly out onto Interstate 10 toward Tucson.

Kate watched the landscape rush by while Cole kept one eye on the rear-view mirror. "It's got a different feel down here," she said.

"It's slower. They don't like us Phoenix folk much."

"Why not?"

"They think all we care about in Phoenix is money, about getting ahead. They think we don't have much respect for the desert or its history."

"That true?"

"Absolutely."

"So what do you guys think of Tucson?"

"It's more relaxed, unhurried. Nice if you like that sort of thing."

"You seem more wired than relaxed—most of the time."

Cole didn't answer, he was thinking about the Camaro behind them.

"I've got an idea," he said. "It's already mid-afternoon. Instead of driving past Tucson and trying to find someplace to stay in Willcox, why don't we stay with a friend of mine down here? We can get an early start in the morning."

"Fine with me. Is he in Tucson?"

"Just west, near Three Points. He's a bit of a hermit, but a good guy. Jimmy Stamps. I was in the Army with him. First Gulf War."

Halfway thru Tucson, the freeway split east and west. Cole took the right fork heading west and kept one eye on his mirror. The maroon Camaro followed far behind, hanging back and hiding behind other traffic.

Twenty minutes out of Tucson, the high desert sprang to life. Spring rains brought a carpet of green desert grass and new growth to the Palo Verde trees. Clumps of yellow brittlebush bloomed in the warm weather.

Kate took in the view. "I can see why your friend would want to live out here, it's gorgeous."

"That's not it. He just doesn't like people. Most of them, anyway."

When they reached a fork in the road with a half-dozen businesses the locals called Three Points, Cole slowed and took a dirt road heading back north. The Camaro faded from sight in his mirror.

"You guys were in the Gulf War?" Kate asked,

"The first one. When we got back, Jimmy had a little trouble adjusting. He used to live near me in Phoenix, we'd go out and drink too much. Jimmy drank so much it got him in trouble with Josie."

"His wife?"

"Nice girl, Josie. Anyway she got sick of him coming home drunk and fighting with her. One night he came home from drinking and passed out on the bed. So she put a sheet over him, took a needle and thread and sewed the top sheet to the mattress. He said it must have taken her three hours. Then she took a cast-iron skillet and beat the crap out of him."

"Ooh, I like her."

"I'm afraid you won't get to meet her. By the time he got out of the sheet, she'd taken the car and all her clothes and left him. He moved down here after that and took up gunsmithing. He's a whiz at building custom rifles."

They pulled up the crushed-granite driveway to a modest house with attached garage. The tiny house was unpainted block, but the wood garage showed multiple-coats of peeling paint in yellow, beige and white.

Kate scanned the deserted surroundings. "It's pretty isolated area to run a business, isn't it?"

"All you need is the UPS truck to come by."

A huge black dog with a bad attitude and mysterious blood-lines pulled her chain tight on its tether. Jimmy came out of the garage and silenced the animal with a wave of his giant arm. He called out to Cole.

"Hey stranger."

Jimmy was a big man, more so at his belt. "How ya been?" He shot a warm smile at his guests.

Cole introduced Kate, but didn't say anything about why they were in the area.

"Texas, eh?" Jimmy asked her.

"Houston," she said.

Jimmy took another look at Cole's face. "She been beatin' on you, Mike?"

"Don't mess with her, she's tough."

Kate sniffed.

"What are you working on these days, Jimmy?" Cole asked.

Jimmy led them to his shop in the garage. Slow-moving fans spun overhead, churning the warm afternoon air. Light streamed in from two skylights and a bank of overhead fluorescent lights. An old Bridgeport mill and a new metal lathe dominated the shop. Outback a compressor clattered on every few minutes, feeding the constant hiss from leaking air lines.

Jimmy pointed at a rifle barrel chucked in the lathe. "I'm building a lot of long-range stuff these days, mostly for the benchrest boys. "Big thirties, usually."

"Glad you're busy."

"What brings you down?"

Cole looked at Kate before speaking. "It's alright, we can trust Jimmy."

She nodded.

"Maybe we should talk about it over a beer," Jimmy said. "Makes my mouth work better."

They went inside and Jimmy pulled three cans of Tecate out of the refrigerator. They sat down at the wobbly kitchen table next to an open window over-looking the desert. Yellow buds from blooming Palo Verdes blew in and littered the linoleum floor.

Cole told Jimmy everything, from the two guys warning him away, to the trip to Dealey Plaza and then Tucson. Jimmy listened intently as he drank his beer.

"So you think you can find this rifle?"

"We hope so," said Kate.

"It's worth a shot," Cole said. "If we weren't on to something, why would those two guys come to my office?"

Jimmy agreed. "Seems strange. But the whole Kennedy thing was strange. Anybody who took half-a-look at it could see the government was lying."

"Kate thinks it was the Mafia who ordered the hit."

"Coulda been. Probably never know," Jimmy said. "It's more important to show it wasn't just Oswald." He snorted. "Oswald couldn't have hit a barn door with a shotgun, much less a head shot with that old rifle."

"He was set-up."

Jimmy got up to get another beer. "You tell Kate about your rifle theory?"

"Not yet," Cole said.

She looked at him quizzically. "What theory?"

Jimmy popped opened his can. "Mike thinks it was a Stoner design rifle, one of the first AR-15s. A semi-auto. Whoever shot from the knoll didn't have enough time to cycle the bolt on a bolt-action rifle. Mike thinks there were three knoll shots. First to last, it was only nine seconds, and that includes shots from other buildings."

"So how many shots were fired?" Kate asked.

Jimmy thought a minute. "Six or seven, hard to say exactly. Some were right on top of another so it sounded like one shot, some missed their target completely."

Cole said, "If I'm right, it was an early Colt, or maybe an Armalite rifle. Colt made some sniper rifles for the CIA."

"That would mean the CIA was involved," Kate said. "I've got a hard time believing that."

"They could have allowed it by not getting involved."

"I don't follow."

"If the CIA heard the Mafia had a shooter in Dallas, they could have made it easier for them."

"Or helped them," Jimmy said.

Cole explained. "They changed the parade route to run through Dealey Plaza at slow speed. The press photographer car was eight cars back in the motorcade; usually they're right behind the President. That would eliminate a photo record. Then the Secret Service bodyguards were told to stay off the Limo, normally they rode on the car running boards. The Dallas Police had extra men all along the parade route, but none in Dealey Plaza."

Kate threw up her hands. "I know, it sounds bad."

Cole looked at Jimmy. "Is it alright if we stay here tonight? That way we can get an early start."

"Sounds great, I could use some company." He opened the freezer door and looked inside. "I'll thaw some steaks and we can barbeque dinner."

Cole walked out to his truck and brought their bags in the house. He put Kate's bag in the extra bedroom.

"I'll sleep on the living room couch," he said.

She thanked him and eyed the bathroom. "I think I'll take a quick shower and change, if you don't mind."

She went in her room and closed the door.

Cole put his hand on Jimmy's shoulder and pointed outside. They walked out the front door and down the driveway. Cole looked down the dirt road they'd just come in.

"What's up?" Jimmy asked.

"I need your help. Somebody's followed us down from Phoenix. Two guys in a maroon Camaro, California plates. Couldn't get a look at their faces. They didn't follow me down your road, but I'll bet they're at the interstate waiting for us to come out. I'd like to know who they are."

"That so." Jimmy rubbed his belly and looked off in that direction. "Then first thing in the morning, I think we oughta pay 'em a little visit."

CHAPTER NINE

Michael Cole woke at four am. He rolled off the couch and slipped into a flannel shirt, Levis and boots, then clipped on his holstered .45. Jimmy was already in the kitchen brewing a pot of black coffee. They poured a couple mugs and went outside to stare at the black sky, then they ducked in the shop.

Jimmy sat down on a bar stool. "Should be light about five-thirty."

Cole leaned against the workbench while they drank their coffee. Nobody talked.

Finally Jimmy drained his mug and spoke his mind. "One thing bothers me. How'd these guys get on to you?"

Cole knew where he was going. "Had to be Kate."

Jimmy played with his empty mug. "You sleeping with her?"

"Does it matter?"

"Only if it screws up your judgment."

"I'm not sleeping with her. What's your problem?"

"How much do you know about her?" Jimmy asked

"Not much. She showed up one day about the same time as the two guys. I checked her background through Phoenix PD, nothing came up. She said she chose me because of my book. She did ask around about me in Dallas, maybe somebody noticed."

"Well, somebody knows more about this than you do."

"I'm sure it's not these two clowns," Cole said.

"What's her angle?"

"Meaning what?"

"What's she want out of this?" Jimmy asked.

"Atonement. She wants to make amends for her uncle's part."

"By proving her uncle was there?"

"By proving it wasn't Oswald. Trying to find some good in that."

Jimmy looked skeptical. "Look. Let's say you find this rifle. Let's say it's just like you thought, an AR15, or something built for an assassin. How you gonna prove it was used on Kennedy? Ain't worth a shit without some way to verify it killed the President."

Cole looked down at the floor, thinking Jimmy was quicker than he remembered. "You know how I can prove it. There's only one way."

"That's right. Does Kate know that?"

"No."

"You gonna tell her?"

Cole hesitated. "Maybe when the time is right. To be honest, I'm not sure what's true anymore."

"About your dad?"

"Yeah. I know what he told me, but I can't be sure. He says one thing and the Dallas police say another. I'd like to find the truth—for myself."

"But you need the bullet."

"No, first we need the gun. Let's see if we can find this rifle."

Jimmy stood and went to his gun safe. "We should get going." He spun the dial, opened the door and pulled out a 12 gauge Remington pump.

"You got any zip ties?" Cole asked.

Jimmy took some long nylon ties off the shelf and then went back to close the gun safe. "I've got a Mossberg twelve if you want it."

"No, I'll stick with my .45. Just give me a wakeup stick, something like an axe handle."

Jimmy put the shotgun down and went to the back of the garage. He returned with a pickaxe that looked like it had earned its keep. He tapped the well-used head off and handed Cole the heavy hickory handle.

Cole hefted it, it was about a yard long and beefy enough for the task. He checked the house, Kate was still asleep and he didn't want to tell her what was going on, not yet. They went out on the driveway and looked up at the blue-black sky. The stars were fading. Cole checked his watch, then pointed down the dirt road.

"Let's walk."

***

Skinny hunched over the Camaro's steering wheel and tried to stay awake, even as dawn showed on the horizon. Staying awake wasn't hard with Chow snoring at full volume in the passenger seat. Chow's head rolled to one side against the passenger window, his mouth hung wide-open as he hacked loudly.

Skinny turned the ignition key on and searched the scratchy AM band for something lively, finally settling on upbeat tunes floating in from close-by Mexico.

Their Camaro sat deep behind an out of business gas station on the Interstate. They could see a half mile or more down the dirt road where Cole's Tahoe had disappeared the day before. Skinny knew it was still down there; he'd cruised up after dark with headlights lights out and seen the Tahoe parked in front of the only house on the dead-end road. They crept back and waited in the shadows. There was only one way out of there and this guy wasn't going to get past them.

"Yeah, that's right, guero, you ain't get past Chewy Martinez. Maybe I whip-up on your ass some more, you don't listen to me an' Chow when we give you the word. No, no, no, my friend. You over there fucking that whore we tole you to stay away from. You in big trouble. You got Chewy and Chow on your ass."

Skinny slapped the dashboard with two hands, keeping time to the music and singing off-key.

"*No sé si el corazón peca, Llorona; en aras de un tierno amor.* Shit, I am really hungry, man. You hungry?"

Skinny turned to his seatmate and jabbed his elbow into Chow's thick arm. "Hey Chow. Wake up. It's getting light out there. Go see if that store's open yet and get us some donuts."

Chow grunted and turned away. Skinny went back to singing and playing the dashboard. Chow just started to snore when the Camaro's windshield exploded in a shower of glass.

***

WHAM!

Cole swung the axe handle and slammed the windshield again.

WHAM!

"Hey!" Chewy grabbed his pistol off the floor and swung open the driver's door. "Hey you mother—"

Jimmy stepped from behind the Camaro and stuck his shotgun muzzle in Skinny's face. "Mornin' boys."

Skinny froze in place with one foot out of the car.

"Just drop that poodle shooter on the ground." Jimmy motioned with the shotgun. Skinny let go of the Glock and Jimmy kicked it away. "Now get out, both of you."

Cole leveled his HK at Chow as he got out the passenger side.

"Let's step behind the car a moment."

Skinny and Chow looked at each other but didn't move. "Hey, we ain't done nothin' wrong here, gabacho. You can go fuck yourself."

Jimmy swung the shotgun around and pointed at the front tire.

BOOM!

The Camaro slumped on its shredded flat tire as Jimmy racked the shotgun to chamber another shell. He swung the barrel back at Skinny's chest. "Don't piss me off, boys, I ain't had my breakfast yet. Get behind the car and put your hands on your head."

The smell of gunpowder hung heavy in the damp morning air.

They shuffled to the rear and stood with hands on head while a Mexican polka played loudly on the car radio. Jimmy pointed the shotgun at them while Cole searched their pockets. Skinny had a wallet with three hundred-dollar bills and California driver's license.

Cole held up the cash. "These look familiar. I'm taking them back, if you don't mind. You still owe me two hundred, asshole."

Chow's pocket's held a wad of twenties, Cole left it. Neither man had a cell phone. Cole threw the wallet on the ground and prodded Skinny in his ribs with the pick handle.

"Martinez, is it? Tell me Mister Martinez, who's paying you to follow us?"

Skinny stood with hands on head and said nothing.

"No comprende?"

Cole turned to Jimmy. "These are the two guys who busted up my office."

He went to the ignition for the keys and opened the trunk. He threw some loose clothes to one side and searched the trunk corners. Then he checked the Camaro's back seat. Cole pointed at the car. "Nothing in there but stale french fries and candy wrappers."

"Ask the big guy," Jimmy said.

Cole looked over at him. "Chow doesn't talk. Somebody cut out his tongue."

Jimmy thought about that a minute. "Then ask Martinez again."

Cole stepped up and thumped Skinny's thigh muscle with the hickory handle. Skinny flinched.

"Who's paying you guys?"

No one spoke.

Cole swung again at Skinny's leg, harder this time.

"Ow!" Skinny bent sideways and almost fell over. "You mother…"

"Lemme hit 'em, Mike," Jimmy said. "You swing like a girl."

"Ok, give me a minute." Cole paced back and forth with the axe handle resting on his shoulder, his HK45 holstered on his hip. "Now, you see my problem, don't you? My friend here wants to hurt you. Personally, I don't like violence. Why don't you tell me who your boss is and we can all go for pancakes?"

Skinny and Chow stood silent, looking straight ahead, hands on their head.

Jimmy motioned with his raised shotgun. "I don't think they like that question."

Cole stopped pacing. "OK, let's try this one. Which one of you guys kicked me in the face at my office?"

Skinny pointed at his friend. "Not me, man. That was Chow."

Cole dropped the axe handle on the ground and swung hard with his fist, hitting Chow square in the nose. Chow's head rocked back no more than an inch. Blood ran out both nostrils and down his face. His eyes glared but he didn't make a sound.

Damn.

Cole shook his wrist and picked up the pick handle. "Hey, I'm starting to like this. One more chance. Who hired you guys?" he asked again.

"Fuck you."

Cole swung the axe handle viciously at Skinny's thigh, stepping into the swing like he was going for center-field fence. Skinny screamed and crumpled to the ground, clutching his leg and cursing Cole's mother.

"What'd you think?" Cole asked Jimmy.

"That's better. But I don't think you broke it yet."

"No, I mean do you think we're gonna learn anything from these two?"

Jimmy shrugged. "Dumb and dumber? They ain't gonna help us none."

Cole agreed. He picked Skinny's Glock off the ground and stripped it down to the frame. He stuck the barrel and loaded magazine in his pocket and tossed the rest on the roof of the old gas station.

"Now what?" Jimmy asked.

"Let's put em in the car."

With a little prodding and a lot of protest, they got Skinny and Chow seated back in the Camaro. Cole used the fat nylon zipties to fasten their wrists to the steering wheel. Then they closed the car door on a stream of curses.

He checked his watch. "We better go back to the house and get Kate. We should get on down the road."

Jimmy thumped on the roof of the car. "How long you want to leave 'em here?"

"Give me a half-day head start, and then call the Sheriff. There's gotta be a warrant on these two somewhere."

"You got it."

They walked back to the house under a brightening sky.

***

When they got back to the house, Jimmy disappeared into his shop. Cole went inside and sat at the kitchen table with Kate. She held her cup of coffee aloft with one hand.

Her eyes narrowed. "Where've you two troublemakers been?"

"Jimmy had a six am yoga class."

"Is that right?"

"We didn't want to wake you so early."

"Considerate. I thought maybe it was a donut run."

"Sorry, we should have brought you something."

"You're up to no good." She studied his face. "You look far too happy."

He hesitated. "I didn't want to worry you, but the guys who trashed my office followed us down here."

She raised her hand to her mouth.

He told her where they'd been and most of what happened, leaving out the interrogation. He studied her face as he talked, looking a clue, any clue.

She seemed concerned but not scared.

"What the hell? Did they say anything?" she asked.

"Nope. It's not that they were too smart, I think they were well paid."

"What if they come by here? What about Jimmy?"

89

"The Sheriff will take care of them. He and Jimmy are tight, old hunting buddies. But you and I are leaving; we can get something to eat on the road."

"Good. I'm all packed, let's go."

Jimmy walked in the kitchen as they were getting ready to leave. "All set?" he asked.

"Thanks for the help, Jimmy. I'm sorry to leave you with a mess," Cole said.

"Don't worry about it. I still owe you."

They drove out the dirt road, slowing as they got near the Interstate and the maroon Camaro. Cole looked, it hadn't moved. He drove past and headed east toward Willcox.

Kate stared out her window and didn't speak. Cole glanced over, but left her alone with her thoughts. Miles clicked by in silence. They were almost to Tucson when he reached over and touched her arm.

"Hey, you ok?"

She gave him a weak smile. "I hope I didn't get you into something too dangerous."

"Don't worry about me."

She sighed. "I can't help thinking I'm being selfish. This whole thing doesn't seem like it's worth the trouble anymore."

"You didn't twist my arm. I've got a lot at stake in this. It's nothing you did."

"I guess," she said. "Just be careful."

CHAPTER TEN

Cruising at 41,000 feet, the Cessna Citation II was loafing at 420 miles per hour. The Citation didn't look like the business jet it started life as, and was not equipped in the same manner. The normal white exterior was painted the same flat-black paint as US Customs Citation jets, but this jet was not from the Customs Department. If it was mistaken for one that would be fine, it might ward off any intrusive questions.

The jet belonged to the Justice Department, Management Division, but the only passenger on board was a subcontractor to a Virginia agency contracted by Justice.

The subcontractor engaged in work that bore little resemblance to the government's original goal of insuring tranquility, providing defense, or promoting the general welfare. The sub-agency's assignment was to do the job expected, by whatever means were necessary, with the understanding that sometimes it took an application of grease and sometimes an insertion of dynamite. This jet and its passenger were from the dynamite division.

Three of the original seven seats were removed to leave space behind the pilot. A six-foot metal rack occupied the empty space, and a long aluminum case was strapped to the rack. Beside it sat a black duffle bag, no logos, no name tag.

The single passenger sat in the rear-most seat of the remaining row. It was his peculiar habit. He sat all the way in the back, like a gunfighter in a western saloon, so he could watch the room and keep anyone from slipping behind him. His name was Grant Whelen and gunfighter was an accurate comparison.

Whelen poured hot liquid from a thermos into his Styrofoam cup and sipped slowly. 'Tea with honey' was what he'd told the pilot. Those were the only words spoken for the duration of the flight from Virginia.

The pilot checked the digital readout of the aircraft's position in latitude and longitude. The Citation's custom electronics processed his flight plan, noted wind speeds at varying altitudes and determined ground tracks. All of which gave him the ability to fly without making contact with curious ground controllers, if need be. Before leaving Virginia, the pilot punched in coordinates for the flight from Dulles to Tucson International.

The sun rose behind them as the Citation made its approach. The pilot dropped his airspeed and then the landing gear. They were on the ground in minutes. The jet taxied to a hanger area adjoining National Guard and military aircraft maintenance.

When the jet door opened, Grant Whelen emerged carrying his black duffle. He blinked in the bright sunlight and slipped on a pair of aviator glasses. Mid-thirties, he wore his blonde hair cropped close to his scalp. He was serious and focused, lean and hard, like he belonged in the cockpit of an F-16.

Two men greeted him at the hangar with a beige Hummer H2. One of them retrieved the aluminum rifle case from the jet and placed it in the rear of the vehicle. Whelen looked at the Hummer with a touch of disdain.

"Not exactly subtle, is it?"

"You may need to get offroad a bit."

He looked it over. "With those tires?"

"Ground clearance will be your problem, not traction. The roads can be a bit rough if they're not paved."

Whelen pulled a holstered Sig 229 from the duffle bag and clipped it behind his right hip, then threw the bag in the passenger seat. "What's the latest?"

They handed him a map marked-up with black felt-tip and GPS coordinates. "Michael Cole spent the night here; he's driving a silver Chevy SUV, a late-model Tahoe. It hasn't moved all night. His tail is parked in a maroon Camaro at the Interstate. Two guys, we think, right here." He put his finger on the location.

Whelen studied the map, then pointed at a written notation. "That his plate number?"

"Yeah, Arizona plates."

"And the transponder?"

"Working great. The pickup box is between the seats." He pointed inside the Hummer.

"What's its range?"

"Sixty miles."

"How far to the subject?"

"About forty miles to a fork in the road called Three Points. No traffic besides the Border Patrol, but there's a lot of them. Even so, the area is pretty desolate."

Whelen climbed in the Hummer and rolled down the window. "Desolate is good."

He got out of the airport and on the interstate going west, opening it up to eighty when the traffic thinned. Minutes clicked by at speed, then he saw the Three Points sign and a speed limit change. He slowed but almost missed it. Whelen pulled in the corner store to grab a quick something to eat, then went outside to locate the Camaro and its passengers. He spotted them across the street, still parked and waiting for Cole.

He listened to the constant tone from his pickup unit. The Tahoe hadn't moved either.

Whelen drove his Hummer to the last parking spot at the Three Points corner store to keep an eye on things. He pulled an apple and a banana out of the paper bag, watching the locals pull in and out as he ate. His compatriot was correct, every-other vehicle seemed to be a green and white Border Patrol truck. Whelen wasn't concerned about them, he had all the Washington ID he needed, even a get-out-of-jail-free 800 phone number.

Half-way through his Granny-Smith, the transponder pickup changed its tone. Whelen adjusted the dial and watched the road. In a couple minutes the warbling tone turned shrill. He saw a silver Tahoe pull out of the dirt road and head east on the highway. The signal quieted down as the vehicle disappeared down the highway.

Whelen started his truck and waited for the Camaro to pull out and follow Cole. It didn't move. He waited three more minutes and then drove across the street and pulled behind the car for a closer look. It didn't look like they planned to follow their quarry. He needed to know why.

Whelen stepped out of the Hummer and removed his Sig. He held it barrel down and close to his leg as he approached from the rear. He saw two men in the front seat through the rear window. He raised his weapon as he reached for the door handle, then he stepped away without touching anything.

Both men slumped forward like cheap rag dolls, all four hands lashed to the steering wheel. Blood oozed from a small-caliber bullet hole in each man's temple. Whelen scanned the area for anyone watching, then returned to his Hummer.

He got back on the highway and sped west after Cole's Tahoe and the fading tone, cursing his luck.

Damn it.

This was an unexpected complication. Either it was Michael Cole's work or there was another player in the game. From what he knew, execution wasn't Cole's style.

So.

Another player.

But who?

***

Cole skirted Tucson's southern edge until they connected with Interstate 10 continuing east. When they were almost clear of town, Cole took an exit south labeled Truck Stop. He stopped in front of a wood building dwarfed by a faded, billboard-sized RESTAURANT sign directly overhead.

"I've got to eat something," he said.

They entered the café and slid in a red-vinyl booth. Most of the clientele were hunched at the counter eating biscuits with white gravy. Fresh coffee aroma mixed with the smell of cooked grease.

They examined their menus and waited for service. Cole made his choice and looked around the room, thinking about Tucson fifty years ago. The cafe probably hadn't changed much, it certainly looked like 1960 with its chipped Formica table tops.

Cole put his elbows on the worn table and leaned forward to talk. "Joe Bonanno lived here for decades, you know. The big Mafioso. He raised his kids in Tucson, did some time in an Arizona prison, too."

"When's that?" Kate asked.

"He was here in the sixties on, maybe the shooter and your uncle stayed somewhere he arranged."

"Maybe." Kate looked around. She seemed more interested in the pancakes at the next table.

He raised an eyebrow. "What's it gonna be? Protein or carbs?" he asked.

She looked back at him. "Sorry?"

"Are you an egg person or a pancake person?"

She sat a little straighter in her chair. "Do I look like a pancake person to you?"

He buried his nose in the menu. "I'm not touching that."

"What's that mean?"

He looked up innocently. "It means you look fabulous, whatever you're eating is working. Keep it up."

"Nice save, Michael Cole."

A well-worn waitress arrived at their table with a note pad and a steaming pot. "Coffee?

They nodded and she poured them both a cup, then pulled a pencil out of her hair bun. Cole ordered sausage with biscuits and gravy, Kate ordered a cheese omelet.

After the waitress left, Cole leaned forward. "You really wanted the pancakes, didn't you?"

"I did not."

"I saw you staring at those blueberry pancakes over there."

"Is that right, mister sausagebiscuitgravy," she said.

"Don't denigrate my Southern health food," he said.

"How long do you think you'll live eating white flour and animal grease?"

"Long enough. And when I die it will be with a smile."

Her face fell at the mention of death. "Just don't die before your time."

"You worried?"

She paused. "A little. I didn't plan on anyone coming after us. Kinda creepy."

Cole sipped his coffee, thinking of the two guys tied up back in their car. "When this whole thing started, you said something about asking around at the Dallas Police Department.

"Yeah, the Captain there, I think. Couple others."

"Who else did you contact?"

"I called the NRA and the Dallas Fraternal Order of Police. They weren't much help."

"Who gave you my name?"

"Captain Williams."

Cole searched his memory. "I don't know him. Who else might know about your uncle and the assassination?"

"Anyone close to him in the last fifty years, I guess," she said.

"Wife? Girlfriend?"

"He never married. He had a few girlfriends when he was younger, a couple women he lived with for multiple years."

"He had friends, didn't he? A close friend, maybe?"

"I don't know. There were several years we didn't talk to each other. It's only after I got divorced and he was near death that we re-connected. I'm sure he had some poker buddies and some other male friends. Not to mention a hospice worker or two toward the end of his life."

"So it could be anyone," he said.

"Don't you think it's somebody I talked to recently? Like the Dallas Police?"

"Maybe. My dad had a problem with them when he was in Dallas."

"But that was so long ago."

"I doubt that Texas politics has changed that much—not at the police department anyway."

The waitress arrived with their breakfast. She poured them more coffee and left the bill. Cole looked around, the café tables filled up with more travelers.

He spoke between bites. "Let's not worry about how or why. We took care of those two guys, so let's just relax and concentrate on the search—and our time here."

She smiled brightly. "Sounds good to me, Mister Cole."

***

It was noon when Deputy-Sheriff Parker got around to visiting Three Points. Jimmy Stamps told him about the situation and said there was no hurry, but he was close by, just sitting at Maxine's drinking his coffee and waiting for his berry pie, so what the hell. The berry pie could wait.

Parker stood next to the Camaro, his cruiser door wide open and his radio cackling, wondering what he should do first. He was not in a hurry. The dead men inside certainly weren't in a hurry, but they weren't the problem. One problem was the heat building up inside the car. He figured it must be getting worse by the minute. The smell was probably doing the same.

He wanted to do something about that, but he couldn't open the Camaro's windows or doors. Whoever tapped the two fine citizens sprawled in front seat had locked the car and taken the keys with them. So Parker started thinking maybe the car was booby trapped, something the drug runners around there had started doing lately for their own amusement. Jimmy hadn't said anything about locking the car, much less about shooting the two gentlemen. Not that Parker thought that was the case.

Jimmy Stamps and he went way back, and he trusted him, but right then he didn't have enough answers to satisfy the Sheriff, and that was important.

Parker got down on his hands and knees and peered under the car, front and back, left and right, looking for wires or dynamite or packets of C4 or God-knows-what. It all looked perfectly normal under there to him. Rusted, mud caked, oily and dented.

He stood up and scratched his head. Should he call the locksmith or the bomb squad, that was the question.

He called Jimmy Stamps instead and asked him if he'd please come over to help him understand the situation a little better. Jimmy was there in five minutes, his old pickup throwing a cloud of dust behind. Jimmy stepped out, walked over and looked in the driver-side window.

"Damn."

Parker nodded. "Is that a mess or ain't it?"

"It'll do," Jimmy said.

"This how you left them?"

"All but the bullet hole in the head. They were swearing and kicking when we left."

"You and Michael Cole?"

"Yeah. But Michael's not your problem."

"I know. Drugs, then?" Parker asked.

"Nope, I think something more serious," Jimmy said. "These are the guys who trashed his office up in Phoenix."

"Then they followed him to your place. Any idea why?"

"We asked 'em politely, but they wouldn't say."

"Too bad. Guess I hafta get some prints." Parker stepped around the car as if deciding if it was worth the trouble. "How long they been here?"

"Six hours or so."

Parker took his hat off and wiped the brim. "Somebody musta came by after you and finished the job. You hear anything?"

"Nope. But I was in the shop. Couldn't have heard that mouse gun anyway."

Parker checked the hole in Skinny's temple. "Whadda ya think? Twenty-two?"

Jimmy agreed. "Maybe silenced."

Parker leaned on the roof and looked out at the green desert floor. A light breeze blew in their face, strong with fresh creosote. "Gorgeous day, ain't it?"

Jimmy looked out himself. "April and October. Two of the best reasons to live in Arizona."

"That and Maxine's berry pie." Parker peered inside the car again. "Gonna be eighty today. Over ninety in the car. It'll play hell with figuring time of death."

"I got a crowbar and a sledge up at the house," Jimmy said.

"No thanks." He slapped the roof top with his palm, but lightly. "I'm worried she might be booby trapped."

"I doubt they had time to rig a bomb. I'd bet whoever it was just wanted to shut 'em up."

"Probably right."

"Clean job. Locked up the car to delay us, then left no clues lyin' around."

"Likely no prints, either. But I better check." He walked around the back of the car and pointed at the license plate. "California. There's a big surprise. They drove a long way just to take a bullet."

Jimmy shook his head.

"Welcome to Arizona, boys."

CHAPTER ELEVEN

Kate looked up from the road map. "Are we still on Interstate 10?"

"Last time I looked," Cole said.

"How far to Willcox?"

"Not sure. What's the map say?"

She held up the multi-folded paper and shook it. "The map doesn't talk, Michael. All we have up here is paper, and cellulose cannot speak. The GPS talks, but it's stuck away somewhere in the back under all your stuff."

"Do you sense a pattern there?"

She seemed to ponder that. "If you talk too much, you get locked in the trunk?"

"That's the one."

They rode in silence awhile.

Kate asked. "You don't talk much, do you?"

"No."

She turned away and looked out her window. "You're good at it."

An hour and a half out of Tucson, the elevation steadily increased. Flat desert gave way to low hills and gullies cut ragged from the spring rains. Tall saguaro cactus stood everywhere, but wild flowers and low brush threatened to takeover.

The Tahoe flashed by a road sign with mileages listed. Cole calculated quickly. "Half-hour to Willcox. You need to stop for anything?"

"Are you inquiring about the condition of my kidneys or the state of my stomach?"

"Seems a bit early for lunch."

"Then find me a bathroom. And I'm not using the bushes."

When Willcox appeared, they took the business route to an in-town gas station. Cole filled the Tahoe with gas and checked the road map. He was looking off to the north when Kate returned.

"Looks like we need to go this way on Fort Grant road," he said. "Can I see your satellite map details?"

She dug some aerial shots from her bag and compared them to the road map. There were a few discrepancies, but Cole had brought an older map.

"The most likely ranch is east of Fort Grant," he said. "Down here somewhere along the base of Graham Mountain."

"What's Fort Grant?"

"It's where the road ends. Used to be an old army post, last century. Now it's an Arizona prison."

They got back in the Tahoe and made their way through Willcox. Cole pointed out some weathered buildings along the road. Most were wood-sided, with dull paint peeling from years of desert sun. Their roof lines sagged with age. "See what I mean about not much changing down here. They're not into fashion or keeping up with the neighbors."

"It's nice, though."

Kate looked more relaxed than he'd seen her before, more comfortable with him. "Can I ask you something?" she said.

"Is it personal?"

"Absolutely," she said.

"I prefer females," he said.

She laughed. "I know that, I can feel it."

"Then what is it?" he asked.

"You carry a gun. When those two guys came to your office and beat you up, why didn't you stop them?"

He didn't look at her. "I wasn't carrying a gun right then."

"You were a soldier and a policeman. You know how to defend yourself, but you didn't have a gun?"

"It's complicated," he said.

"I thought you were a simple guy."

They stopped at Fort Grant highway and turned north. Cole considered his answer.

"My dad, when he was near death two years ago, he asked me not to carry a gun anymore. He was worried about me getting shot. I told him I wouldn't carry. How can you deny a dying father's wish?"

"I can understand that."

He continued. "I'd never needed to draw the weapon all the years I carried it. So I stopped thinking it was necessary."

"Why'd you change your mind?"

"Getting mugged by those two guys. I thought if I avoided trouble it would leave me alone." Cole shrugged. "I was wrong."

***

The tin mailbox perched gingerly on top of a leaning post at the side of the dirt road. Black letters along one side spelled out Porter Ranch.

Cole asked, "Is this it?"

Kate turned the aerial-view picture in her hand sideways. "I'm not sure."

He pointed at the mailbox. "Somebody must live there. What do you think?"

"Let's try it."

He dropped the truck in gear and continued on.

The dirt road followed the San Francisco River along the base of Graham Mountain as far as they could see. They traveled about four miles at a slow pace, avoiding exposed granite rocks popping out of the winding road. It was slow going after their trip on the highway. The last mile inclined gently, then the road fell away to expose a green valley.

Cole stopped the Tahoe at the crest of the hill. They got out to take in the view. On the far side, red-rock cliffs plunged straight down to a boulder-strewn river. Tall cottonwood trees followed the cliff base on both sides of the meandering waterway.

"Look over there." He pointed in the center of the valley.

A large two-story house stuck out as the one man-made structure among the green. The Victorian style, high-pitched roof extended on all sides to shade 360 degrees of the surrounding porch. One side of the house had a second porch off the second story level.

Cole pointed it out. "Check out that summer sleeping porch. This house has got to be a hundred years old."

They could see old irrigation canals, now dry. New electrical lines strung on poles ran from the main house to a stone structure at the river. Bare-branched trees stood naked in multiple rows.

"It looks like they used to have an orchard down there."

"Let's go look."

They descended into the valley and drove up to the house.

Kate and Cole stepped out and stood in the sunshine and a light breeze.

"It seems deserted." She looked closer. "It's not what I pictured, either."

"Somebody lives here, it's furnished inside." He cupped his hands and called out. "Hello!"

They walked all around the house, noting the cracked windows and sagging doors. The home seemed weather-tight but in need of a fresh coat of its white paint. They hadn't walked all the way around before they heard a vehicle honk twice from the road. They turned to look.

A battered F-250 crested the hill and drove down and over to where they were standing. The pickup stopped and a silver-haired woman stuck her head out the driver's window.

"Hello there," she said. "We're not open yet, if that's why you're here."

Kate and Cole walked over to greet her. Cole checked the contents of the truck bed and the age of the driver. She appeared a bit old to be piloting a pickup full of wood and supplies. The woman looked late sixties or maybe seventy, but leather-skinned and wiry. She climbed out of the truck and slammed the door, glancing at the pistol on Cole's hip.

"Worried about snakes?"

"No mam, just careful sightseers."

"You should be. The rattlers are out sunning. You need to be careful."

"We will."

"You probably read that article in the paper about us," she said. "That reporter was so nice. Are you down from Phoenix?"

"We are." Cole looked at Kate.

"Well, my carpenter quit and he's put me a month behind opening. I'm sorry, we should be renting by now."

"Renting rooms?"

"Our bed and breakfast. Porter Ranch. Not quite ready. Would you like some ice tea? I have some sun-tea brewing and it should be done."

Cole looked again in the bed of the truck. "Let me bring these things in for you. I'm Michael and this is Kate."

"I'm June Porter. That would be wonderful. You can put the wood next to the house, Michael, and the groceries in the kitchen, please. Come with me, Kate, and we'll get the tea off the porch."

The two ladies walked to the house. June Porter was nearly as tall as Kate, certainly as long legged. She moved with a gait that matched the much-younger woman. Cole removed his pistol and locked it in the Tahoe, then pulled and stacked the dozen studs on the shady side of the house. He brought four boxes of groceries inside. June poured dark tea into tall green glasses.

"No ice, I'm afraid." she said. "Not till next week when they get the power done. Diesel generator in the pump house. A lot to do yet."

"That's fine, Mrs. Porter."

"Call me June. I've grown to prefer my tea a bit warm anyway. Sugar?"

They moved to a large interior room with white plaster walls trimmed with dark-stained wood. One wall held a huge fireplace with new mantle installed, carved in the same ornate pattern as the floor boards and wainscot trim. It was dark-stained also but waiting on a coat of varnish. They sat down on newly-upholstered chairs made from the same dark wood.

Cole looked closely at it. "Is this mesquite?"

"It is. With walnut stain."

"You've done a lot of work around here, June," Cole said.

She sipped some of her tea and rested her head on the chair back. "The old place is nothing like it used to be, I'm afraid. My father had an orchard with over 200 fruit and pecan trees."

"How old is the home?" Kate asked.

"It was built it in 1912. We had sixty acres, originally. I grew up here, but we lost the house to the bank after my father took a mortgage for a new roof. We moved on to Sacramento for his health." she said, tapping her breast. "His heart."

"When did you move back?"

"I bought it from an eastern investor in 2001. I've been doing this and that when I can. Most of the time I live in Willcox. My daughter comes to help me, and we hire a worker or two. She'll move in permanent when we open for business."

Kate looked sideways at Cole. "Did anyone live here in the sixties?"

"The house had many owners after my father sold. It sat vacant a long time, and then the 1983 floods did a lot of damage to it. Stripped the valley floor clean. The water even came inside the house. Our old carpet was chock-full of sand and mud. More tea, anyone?" She got up and moved to the kitchen. "I've got some apple pie, if you like."

Cole looked at Kate but she shook her head.

"No thank you," said Cole. "But can we do anything else for you around here?"

She returned with a full glass and sat down. "I have a few things needing tending around here if you want to help. Why don't you spend the night? I have plenty of bedrooms, as you can well see."

"We wouldn't want to impose—"

She held up her hand. "Now don't be running off, you two. I'd love to have you stay with me. We can trade a little work for your room, if you like. And your dinner, I have more than enough. As for chores, that back door sticks and won't open without a good kick."

"That's very kind of you. We'd love to stay and help." Kate said. She winked at Cole. "He's not a scholar but he has a strong back."

June Porter smiled. "That's all we need. There are tools in the rear storage room."

Cole left Kate and June to their conversation in the parlor and went to check the back door problem. It sagged under its own weight and rubbed hard at the bottom edge. He found a Philips screwdriver in the mix of tools on the shelf and removed the screws holding the door hinges to the jamb. He leaned it carefully against the doorway and examined the edge where it rubbed.

At home he would have used his belt sander on the edge, but here he needed older technology with muscle power.

Kate Porter kept enough woodworking tools in the storeroom to build a house and all its furniture, but none of them were power tools. Cole found an old Stanley bedrock plane and adjusted its blade for a thin cut, then set to work with the door between his legs. Shavings curled off and floated to the floor as he stroked. He had most of the material removed when Kate appeared.

"How you doing?" she asked.

"Not bad for a dumb city-boy. Find out anything?"

"She's a wonderful old person, that much I know. But she doesn't know anything about this house in the sixties, I'm afraid. She gave me a tour upstairs."

Cole finished removing material and stood the door up.

"We'll talk outside. Help me hold the door while I put the screws back in."

When the hinges were tight, he swung the door to make sure it cleared the jamb. He tightened the door-handle screws, swept-up and put the tools away.

"Let's walk down to the river."

They took a rutted path through the grassy meadow. Worn tree-stumps poked out of the green grass to greet them, while wildflowers brushed their legs. Cole walked ahead, remembering June's caution on snakes. When they reached the river, Cole turned around and looked at the old house.

"You looked in the bedrooms?" he asked.

"All of them."

"Does anything look like it's been redone—like the walls in any room?"

"No," she said. "Our old house in Houston had plaster walls; I know what it's like to repair. These walls all look original. I suppose there could be damage behind a dresser, there's two rooms with those."

"What about in the ceilings?"

"They're plaster, too, but I didn't check them for damage. We should have brought a metal detector."

"That would work, but you'd find every bracket and pipe." Cole picked up some small rocks and threw them in the river, watching the ripples float downstream with their hopes. "Why don't we come right out and ask her?"

"Ask her what?" Kate asked. "That we want to cut holes in her walls? This is looking like a bad idea."

"Not entirely. We've seen the area, now we need to examine the ownership records around here during 1963. The County Recorder will have that."

"You don't think the rifle's here?" Kate asked.

"I doubt it. I was hoping to find something more obvious. Is there anything your uncle said that we might be missing?"

"He said the rifle's in the wall, in the room where he stayed at the ranch. That's plain enough," she said.

"But not obvious. If it's not in these rooms, maybe this isn't the right ranch. We need to find a better possible location."

Kate sat down on a boulder, picked a wildflower and inhaled its fragrance. "I'm sorry I got you into this, Michael."

"Forget it. Let's go back inside and see what else we can do for June. When I get a chance I'll take a look at the walls in each room."

CHAPTER TWELVE

Grant Whelen reached the Porter mailbox just after sundown. He kept driving, thankful for the ground clearance the Hummer afforded. When the transponder signal hit a fever pitch, he pulled over and parked. He checked his mirror, then removed a pair of Nikon high-power binoculars from his nylon bag.

He walked to the crest of the hill and scanned the valley. In the fading light he could see Cole's silver Tahoe parked alongside a pickup truck. Flickering lights inside the house revealed human shadows in lower-level window curtains. He walked back to the Hummer and sat down.

He checked for a signal on his cell phone, but nothing showed. His daily report would have to wait. He held a flashlight on his unfolded topo map and studied the area. It looked like the dirt road would dead-end before hitting any highways. Cole couldn't elude him by going much further east, he'd have to come back west to where the dirt road hit Fort Grant.

Whelen turned around and drove back the way he came in. After two miles the signal quieted down. He drove off-road as far as possible until the Hummer was mostly hidden, then he turned it around until he had a view of the road through his windshield. He dialed the unit down a notch, figuring he could catch some sleep before morning.

If Cole drove past in the night, the squeal from the passing transponder would wake him up. If not, he'd investigate the situation at dawn.

He didn't know whether they had the rifle or not. He didn't want to tip them off he was after the same thing. He'd follow their vehicle until they stopped somewhere, then he'd break-in and take it. If Cole didn't stop before Phoenix, he'd stop them himself.

The rifle would not get away. If he took possession, they'd triple his fee.

Triple was good.

***

Everyone ate evening dinner by flickering lantern light. The lanterns cast an amber glow on textured walls that felt natural for the old house and its history. The glow extended to both Kate and Cole after consuming a portion of a bottle of Jack Daniels (leftover from the painter's work, June explained).

Their dinner was beef stew, straight from the can but cooked piping hot on her old iron stove using mesquite-wood strips. It was the best meal Cole had eaten in months. His appetite might have come from the whiskey or from the hour he'd spent chopping mesquite for June Porter.

Cole's afternoon examination of the house showed no trace of what they'd come for. If a firearm was hidden there in the sixties, it was long gone. He put the rifle out of his thoughts and concentrated on Kate Marlowe and the moment.

They'd done the few dishes and then reclined in front of the stone fireplace, watching a fire consume a stack of his freshly-split logs.

"It takes the chill off before bed," June explained.

She'd joined them for a while, but begged off early and gone upstairs to bed, leaving them sitting on the overstuffed sofa watching the flames. The only sound was the pop and hiss of burning mesquite, its distinct smoky tang filling the big room.

"You can see why June wanted to come back here," Kate said. "It's so quiet, so beautiful."

"She's amazing, I'll give you that. I couldn't live alone like this."

She glanced over. "But you do live alone."

"Not this alone. I live with a television, two cell phones and the internet. I've got 24 hour news and Chinese takeout when I want it. I've got neighbors. Still, I don't like living alone. But out here you have another level of alone."

Kate asked, "If you don't like living alone, how come you never remarried?"

"I'm not very good at marriage."

"Once bitten—"

"Twice shy. My sister says that's my problem."

"Might be worth trying again," she said.

"Why? I can't think of a good reason."

"To get it right one time."

"Maybe," he said. "Or it might confirm I really am a jerk."

"Don't be so hard on yourself."

He thought. "I don't want to fail at it again."

"You think it was your fault?"

"Probably."

"It takes two in a marriage."

"If you're both reasonable."

"You seem like a reasonable man to me."

Cole stared deep into the flames. "One time, early on, my ex wanted to get some new frilly sheets. Laura Ashley or something, with huge pink flowers all over. I wouldn't let her buy them. I told her real men don't sleep on flowered sheets."

"She left you over sheets?"

He exhaled slowly. "It was one of a thousand paper cuts."

Kate was quiet. "I wasn't that lucky. It was good one day and intolerable the next when I found out he cheated on me. Then the bastard married her."

"Sorry you had to go through that."

"It's history," she said. "Besides, I'm here with you tonight. So far it's a good trade."

"So far?"

Kate toyed with her hair. "It could get better."

Cole placed his hand on her thigh. She was hot from the fire, her flesh firm to the touch. "Where are we sleeping tonight?" he asked her.

"June said there were twin beds in two bedrooms in the back, and to take what we need."

"How many do we need?" he asked.

"One."

Cole got up and stoked the fire. He sat down closer to Kate, pressing against her, heady from her closeness. She looked at him and put her head back on the couch, lips parted.

He brushed her hair from her face. He kissed her mouth deeply and her neck softly, his hand exploring her willing breasts. Kate's breathing deepened until it came in short gasps.

Finally she broke away. "Take me upstairs."

In their room they wrestled with clothes and then each other, fiercely at times, desperate for passion denied. He caressed her body, she touched his heart. Minutes and memories flew by, finally serenity settled on them both.

In the dark, there was only steady breathing and a distant owl. A thin moon cast faint outlines of their bodies on the far wall. Cole held Kate in his arms, marveling at her sweet smell and soft skin. He was almost asleep when his old lament floated to the top.

Should have let her get those sheets.

***

Jimmy Stamps tried Cole's cell again, but still couldn't get an answer. He cursed, thinking he should have arranged something with his friend to call, they knew service was spotty in southern Arizona. Cole could have called Jimmy's land line before he disappeared off the grid.

Jimmy pan fried some ground beef and microwaved a potato for dinner. He let Dixie in the house, she waited patiently for the table scraps she knew would come at the end of his meal. When Jimmy was done eating, he scraped the rest of his plate in her bowl along with her regular food.

Jimmy knew Cole was operating on too little information. He needed to know somebody killed the two men in the Camaro. Judging by the body count so far, killing came quick and easy to them.

Jimmy washed his plates and then checked his email. It wasn't much, but it was his social life, the only social contact besides Barb. They had a date every Saturday night, schedules permitting. But tonight Jimmy got on the internet, eventually ending up at AR15 forum.

A recent topic on JFK caught his eye. Grassy knoll. Sniper rifle auction. Fiftieth anniversary. He read all the posts. Some said it was worth a million dollars. Some said five million.

How the hell would they know?

Kate and Cole were on to something after all. Something bigger than they knew. Jimmy tried to put it out of his mind, but he couldn't. The fact that those two died in the Camaro gave credibility to Cole's quest.

Jimmy had his own thoughts about JFK and some of his policies, but he knew one thing. Everything went in the toilet after Kennedy was killed. The distrust of government, the loss of hope, it all started with Dealey Plaza and the cover-up lies. America's light dimmed that day in Dallas.

If Jimmy got a chance to throw it back in their face, he damn well would.

CHAPTER THIRTEEN

It was the smell that got them up, a cinnamon pumpkin something that floated up the stairwell and into their room.

"What's she baking now?" Kate wondered.

They dressed quickly and moved downstairs. June stood at the hot stove, pouring pancake batter in a black skillet.

She smiled at them. "Pumpkin pancakes, my specialty. Honey or boysenberry preserves, your choice."

Kate inhaled. "Smells wonderful."

"I've already had mine, you two sit down."

She cooked them breakfast and told them stories of her childhood over coffee. "Dad had a small gold mine in the cliff, that's how he paid for a lot of this. It didn't last, though. The vein went dry."

After they had eaten they cleaned the kitchen.

"Are you going back to Phoenix today?" June asked."

"Yes, after we look around a little more."

"Are you thinking of buying a place down here? The prices are very low now."

"No, just sightseeing. Kate's uncle passed through here fifty-years ago and loved the area. She's retracing his steps; she thinks he stayed at a ranch somewhere around here."

June said, "I don't know of any other ranches. Most went out in the fifties."

"Are the ranch buildings still standing?" Cole asked.

"The flood took the only one I know of. You might ask the businesses around Fort Grant, some of those have been here for fifty years." She paused. "Is there something special about the place you're looking for?"

"Memories, I guess," Kate said.

"Memories are important. I think of my husband a lot. I wish he was still with me."

"Aren't you afraid to live here alone, June?"

"No, not anymore. Most people don't travel this far off the beaten path. If the wrong fellow does happen by, I always have Nelly." She pointed at the kitchen.

"You have a dog? Kate asked.

"My shotgun. Nothing special, just an old twenty gauge, as I remember. I keep it in the pantry. Haven't had to use it, not once. I'm not even sure if Nelly's loaded."

"You should know if it's loaded, June," Cole said. "Would you like me to check it for you?

"Michael's an expert on firearms," Kate said.

"Is he?"

"That's what he does, he works with firearms and ballistics."

June sat in a rocking chair. "Then let me ask you something. I gave my shotgun a name to make it less threatening. Do you think guns can have personalities?"

Cole hesitated. "I've never thought about that. I suppose they work well with their owner or they don't. Some fit your hand like a glove and shoot where you point. Some aren't accurate at all. A gun that doesn't hit where you aim it is pretty-much useless."

"So guns can be good or guns can be bad. Is that what you mean?"

"Yes, mam."

June rocked a moment. "But can they be evil?"

Cole struggled to find a polite answer. "Guns can certainly do evil in the wrong hands."

"No, I mean can the weapon itself be evil?"

Cole shook his head, not comfortable with her questions. "I don't believe that's possible. No."

"Do you believe in evil?" June looked at Cole specifically.

"I do," Cole said. "I've seen enough of it."

She rocked a little more in her chair. "Then please, I'd like you to take the gun away from here."

"Why would you give up Nelly? You should have something for protection."

"No, Michael, not Nelly, the rifle. I want you to take it away. That's what you came for, isn't it? I heard you talking about a rifle yesterday."

Cole couldn't think of the right words. He just looked at Kate.

June continued. "My carpenter found a hidden rifle when we repaired the bedroom floorboards. I don't know how it got in the wall, but it was there a long time. My workman got it out, it was a bit rusted so he cleaned it all up. He put it in the workroom on the top shelf. Said he was going to get some ammunition for it."

"Did he fire it?"

"He never got the chance. He was killed on the road that same evening when a car hit him head-on. That was nearly nine months ago."

"Are you saying the rifle is still here?"

"I'm afraid to touch it. I'm afraid to let anyone touch it. It's evil. My Siamese cat used to sleep in the storeroom, but he wouldn't go inside after we put the gun in there. Then he ran away."

"Surely that's a coincidence; maybe the oil smell bothered him."

"I don't think so. There's a Coral Vine outside of that storeroom wall, it's bloomed every spring for the last twelve years without fail. Hundreds of pink flowers, all summer long. This year it withered and died. That rifle is evil, Michael. Take it out of the house, and please, be careful what you do with it."

He hesitated. "June, are you sure?"

"Please. Take it."

Cole and Kate walked back to the storeroom to look. Cole pulled a stool up to the wall of shelves and stood on it, feeling around on the top shelf. He closed his hand on cold steel.

"It's here."

He pulled the weapon off the shelf, stepped down and placed it on the workbench. It was covered in dust. Cole examined it as he cleaned it with a rag. There were traces of rust on the receiver, but it looked in good condition. The plastic stock was green.

"Amazing," Cole said. "Just amazing."

It looked like a Vietnam-era M16 with a stubby scope on its carry handle. The handguard was smooth and triangular shaped. The telescopic sight was a military model. Cole held it up and sighted through, it seemed like three or four power.

The barrel looked unusual to him. It was stainless steel, longer and fatter than normal and did not have a flash hider. Cole dropped the magazine; it was a standard-issue steel twenty-round. He searched the grey receiver for a manufacturer name but none was stamped. No serial number either.

Strange.

A firearm with no serial number was illegal; a firearm that never had a number engraved couldn't be a production rifle.

Kate watched him look it over. "That's gotta be it, right?"

Cole set it down on a workbench. "It's from the right era—pre Vietnam—but it's not a service rifle. It looks like a sniper's rifle to me but you wouldn't use an automatic for sniping."

"Can you trace it?" she asked.

"There's no serial number. Never had one."

"What does that mean?"

"Not sure. Green Berets were in Vietnam early, before the war started. Maybe they made something special for them."

He thought a minute.

Or the CIA.

"Let me check inside."

He removed the takedown pin from the lower receiver and then the front pivot pin, splitting the receiver in two pieces. He pulled back on the charging handle, removed the bolt carrier and examined it.

"Not chrome plated," he said. "So it's pre-1966."

He checked the hammer and sear.

"It's a semi-auto, not full automatic. They made AR-15's in '63, so it could be one of them, but modified."

He re-assembled the rifle as he talked. "It's not a field weapon, it's some sort of specialty rifle, something the CIA boys could use for execution, whatever. Perfect for a sniper. You don't lose cheek weld with a semi-auto."

"I don't understand," Kate said.

"On a bolt-action rifle, you load and unload the cartridge by opening and closing the bolt with one hand. The semi-auto does it for you, using the pressure from the fired bullet. One trigger pull, one shot and an automatic chambering of the next round."

Kate touched the rifle stock. "So this ended up in my uncle's hands."

"You said he helped train the Bay of Pigs forces in the Everglades. He could have got it down there."

"Or maybe the CIA gave it to their Mafia connections," she said.

"Let's put it in the truck."

Cole took it out the back door and over to his truck. He set the rifle in the back and returned to the house for their bags. He started to throw them in the rear, then unzipped his duffle and put the rifle inside. He closed the truck and rejoined the women.

Kate said goodbye to their host. Cole joined them as June rambled on, apparently starved for company. Cole turned on his phone while they talked.

"Oh, you won't get any service down here," June said. "You need to drive up to the top, and then go left a half-mile. That's what I do."

"Thank you."

"Please come back in a few months, you two. We'll have electricity and better food," June said.

"We rather liked it this way, June, "Cole said. "Couldn't have been better."

Kate waved as they drove out, the Kennedy rifle stashed carefully in the duffle behind their seats.

***

Grant Whelen woke before sunup with a serious urge to urinate and a newly-formulated plan. He zipped up his jacket, got out of the Hummer and walked a few paces to the rear to relieve himself. First light revealed a layer of dew on the desert terrain. He opened the back of his

Hummer, ate a few bites of stale roll and drank water as he listened for traffic on the dirt road.

Satisfied, he yanked the long rifle case out and set it on the ground. He popped the lid and removed a military-issue Barrett M107. He installed a ten-round magazine filled with black-tipped .50-caliber M2 cartridges, then checked the Leupold scope for tightness.

Whelen placed the case and rifle carefully back in the Hummer and drove toward the old house in the valley.

The transponder pick-up screamed at the top of the hill. He shut it off and parked on one side of the road. He grabbed his binoculars and strode to the crest as the sun broke the horizon. Whelen crouched and moved closer, then lay prone to glass the scene below. Jagged rocks dug into his elbows and knees as he scanned the valley, but he dismissed the pain. His pulse was elevated but his breathing slowed as he focused on the task at hand.

The only thing he saw moving below was an occupant in the home's kitchen. Whelen checked his watch, 6:10. He settled in to wait.

At 7:42 Michael Cole walked out of the house with a firearm in hand. He leaned the rifle against the Tahoe fender as he unlocked the doors. Whelen dialed-up the power of the Nikons and studied the piece before it disappeared in the back of the truck. Early handguard. Grey receiver. No forward-assist. Fat barrel. And what the hell was that scope...yes, the Odelft three-point-six.

It was not the 1963 Remington Fireball he expected to see, but another sixties-era sniper rifle.

Son of a bitch.

He'd seen one three-years ago in Virginia. He knew a human body hit with this rifle would suffer significant tissue damage, but a headshot would explode like a jug of water from the hydrostatic pressure. The CIA used them in the early sixties for assassination in Laos and North Vietnam

If there was a better weapon in 1963 to shoot a President traveling in an open vehicle from fifty meters, Whelen didn't know what it might be. By current standards, he thought, it was a bit of a relic. Now an assassin with a Barrett fifty could kill a man standing a thousand-meters away.

Is this a great country or what?

He ran back to his Hummer and backed down the road until he could turn around, then drove west until he had a half mile clear view.

He angled the Hummer in the middle of the dirt road to block oncoming traffic and shield him from view. He removed the Barrett, dropped the monopod and its bipod, then aligned it pointing straight down the dirt road. He lay flat, racked the bolt and chambered a round. He put his ear protection on and focused the scope on the crest of the road bed where Cole would appear.

Whelen was zeroed at fifteen-hundred yards. All he needed now was a fat, dumb, Chevy Tahoe.

CHAPTER FOURTEEN

Cole pulled out of the valley and checked for a cell signal again. He couldn't get anything so he turned east and followed the road higher.

"She said to go a half mile," Kate said. "Who you calling?"

"Susan," he said.

She looked over at him. "That your girlfriend?"

Cole got to the top of the hill and stopped in a wide area. "Sorry, Susan's my sister. I need to talk to her."

He found cell service and three waiting messages from Jimmy Stamps. He stared at the phone, thinking something must have gone wrong. A message a year was the most he'd ever got from his reclusive friend. Now he had two from yesterday and one from early morning. He retrieved the first message and listened to it play.

What the hell?

"What's up?" Kate asked him.

Cole frowned. "Nothing good."

***

Whelen thought he might have miscalculated. Maybe Cole was heading the other way.

Impossible.

His maps showed the only exit was past him, and that wasn't gonna happen. He went back to the Hummer and turned the transponder pickup loud enough to hear from his shooting position. The tone was steady, that was good. If it started fading Cole would be traveling east and he'd have put the Barrett away and follow. That was not good. Things could get messy with close quarters shooting, vehicle damage—even mission failure.

The fifty-caliber solution trumped all others.

Whelen got down in position and waited.

***

Jimmy didn't hear his phone ring. Normally he left it in the house when he worked in the shop, but this morning he had it close by in case his friend called.

At that moment he wouldn't have heard it anyway. He was turning gun-barrel threads with his metal lathe.

He watched the oil-drenched chips fall away, thinking of Deputy Parker. He'd already come by that morning with a few more questions about the Camaro incident. Parker said he wanted to ask Michael Cole a few questions, but understood he was out of reach. It could wait, Parker said. It's just the Sheriff, he apologized.

Jimmy cleaned the chips off his work and checked the cut depth with a thread gauge, then checked fit with the action itself.

Too tight.

He stepped away from the lathe. His concentration was elsewhere. If he kept working he was likely lose a finger or screwup the expensive barreling job.

Jimmy shut down the shop and cleaned his hands with solvent, then soap and hot water. It wasn't all that far to Willcox, he thought. Maybe he should get a little closer to the action. At least he'd feel better. He locked the house, got in his truck and drove to the junction.

***

Cole turned around and headed west to Fort Grant.
"What's wrong?" Kate asked. "What was that message?"
"Jimmy said somebody killed the two guys in the Camaro, right after we left. I can't get anymore information than that because he's not answering."
She didn't look at him. "So we're in danger, too."
"Especially now that we have the rifle. We need to get to Phoenix. When I hit the interstate I'm gonna take another way. Hopefully a safer route."
They drove past the turnoff to June Porter's house and kept moving. Cole tried to decide if the best choice would be wide-open freeways or narrow secondary roads. Neither seemed safe, but he didn't want to drive by Tucson again.
"No one followed us here, did they?" Kate asked.
"Impossible. I was watching, I would have seen them on this long road."
Kate turned around and looked back. "I hope we didn't put June in danger."
Cole didn't say anything; he just gripped the wheel tighter.

***

Whelen relaxed as the transponder tone elevated. He pulled the heavy rifle firmly into his shoulder and watched through the scope.
Come to papa.
The pick-up squealed.

A silver Tahoe crested the rise, framed perfectly against the sky as it moved toward him. The image filled Whelen's lens, his scope crosshairs centered on the grill.

He squeezed off a round.

BOOM!

Recoil slammed his shoulder as the armor-piercing bullet left the barrel with 11,000 foot-pounds of energy, ten times the force of a 44 magnum. The steel-tipped bullet covered the distance in one second and pierced the chevron grill emblem.

Cole's truck rolled to a stop.

Whelen jumped up and put the rifle in the back. He drove toward Cole as fast as the rock-filled road allowed.

***

The engine locked as the boom hit Cole's ears. For a moment he thought his motor blew, but then he realized what it was. He slammed the brakes on his slowing vehicle.

"Get out!" Cole yelled and pointed. "Get in that ditch, now!"

He pushed Kate to leave the vehicle and he did the same. He lay at the side of the road with his pistol out, cursing the futility. His handgun was no match for the rifle ahead of them. He looked far down the road, he couldn't see anything.

"Stay down," he called to her.

There was no place to go. If they stood and ran, one of them would be shot. Someone had chosen the ambush site carefully. He heard the crunch of tires on gravel as a vehicle approached. Then it stopped. He kept his head down. One man or two?

Kate called out, fear in her voice. "Michael!"

"Stay down."

Cole looked up. He could see a beige Hummer with the driver door open. Whoever it was had the cover of his vehicle and a weapon in hand. The Hummer was fifty or sixty yards away. There was no shot for Cole to take, but plenty for him to receive.

"Cole!"

Whoever it was knew his name.

"I can hit the lady from here," the voice said. "If you shoot, she's dead. If you run, you're both dead. All I want is the rifle."

Cole swore under his breath.

He went on. "Leave your weapon on the ground and walk over here, hands on your head."

Cole hesitated, but left the HK in the dirt and walked toward the Hummer. All he could see was a blonde crewcut and a gun barrel. When he got halfway there he saw a raised hand.

"Stop. You have any weapons on you?" Blondie asked.

"No."

"Lift your shirt and turn around."

Cole did.

"Now your girlfriend."

Cole called out. "Kate. Come over here." He turned to the gunman. "She's not armed."

Kate walked over and stood with Cole. She took his hand and squeezed it.

"Sit down, both of you, hands on your head."

They sat down and waited. A tear streaked the dust on Kate's face.

The blonde gunman came out from behind the Hummer. "That rifle isn't worth dying for, but you can, if you insist. Where is it?"

"In the duffle, in the back," Cole said.

Blondie walked past them and over to the Tahoe, watching them both all the while. He kicked Cole's handgun off the road and opened the truck's backend.

He returned with the rifle in one hand and his pistol in the other. He put the rifle in his vehicle and walked over to Kate and Cole, then crouched ten feet away, pistol relaxed in his hand.

"What happens now is up to you. I suggest you sit there until I'm long gone, then start walking. You could be at Fort Grant in a couple hours. When you get there, call a tow truck, not the Sheriff. Because if some deputy with a wife and kids pulls me over, I'll just have to shoot the poor slob in the face. You don't want that on your conscience." He stood up. "It's just an old rifle."

Cole looked at Kate and nodded. "We'll walk out."

Blondie walked back to his Hummer.

Cole called after him. "Wait."

Blondie turned around.

"Who was it?" Cole asked.

He paused at the Hummer's door. "Who sent me? I don't know." He climbed in and rolled down the window. "Who killed Kennedy? I don't care."

Then he drove off.

They sat in the dirt until he was out of sight, then Cole helped Kate off the ground.

"Well, that's that," she said, watching the settling dust.

Cole walked back to the Tahoe and examined the hole in his grill. "Looks like it's time for a new motor."

He picked his HK out of the ditch checked it over. He blew the dirt off, cycled the slide, then stuck it back in his holster. He scanned the area for anyone, anything out of the ordinary. He couldn't help thinking they'd been right about the rifle all along, but now it was a wasted effort.

They helped the wrong people by giving them the rifle. But who?

Who are these guys?

Cole got down on the ground and looked under his truck in the front, then the rear.

Kate watched him search, then asked, "What's wrong?"

Cole mumbled from underneath. "Nothing." He scrambled out and looked in the wheel wells. "They must be tracking us, I'm looking for a sending unit, anything."

Finally he stood up. "Nothing I can find. Let's go up the road where we got cell service."

"Why? We can walk this way." She pointed to Fort Grant.

Cole checked his wrist watch. "I want to try Jimmy again. And we can get some help out here by calling Willcox. We need a tow truck."

Kate crossed her arms. "Then I'm staying here."

"Suit yourself, just watch out for rattlers." He only managed three strides.

"Wait, I'm coming with you." She got in step. "Why are you calling Jimmy?"

"He warned me, now I need to warn him."

"You think this guy will do anything to hurt him?"

"No. I think he got what he came after, he'll probably want to leave the state now." Cole said.

"Then why…"

"Because I'm not sure. I'm not sure of anything."

CHAPTER FIFTEEN

Jimmy's cell was buried deep in his shirt pocket. The phone was on vibrate, otherwise he wouldn't have heard it over Toby Keith. He kept one hand on the steering wheel as he fished it out.

"This is Jimmy."

He listened while Michael Cole explained what happened on the road.

"Damn, that's hard to believe...Sounds like you had it...Uh huh. What's he drivin'?...That foo-foo model, the H2?...What's this guy look like?...Uh huh. You better get your truck out of there, lest somebody strip it tonight. There's a tow truck in Willcox at Baxter's Garage. I'd call them. How long ago did this happen?...I will. Talk to you in a few hours." Jimmy hung up.

Did he go east or west?

He checked the time on his phone. An hour had passed. Which meant the shooter was either close to New Mexico or driving straight at him.

The Benson exit was three miles ahead. He stepped on the gas and watched oncoming traffic for a boxy beige Hummer.

Jimmy's pickup was a seventies three-quarter ton with a breathed-on 351 Cleveland motor. It leapt to ninety and he held it there until the freeway exit. He crossed the overpass and started down the ramp pointing back to Tucson. He pulled off the ramp before entering the highway and sat, waiting for the Hummer to fly by.

He knew he might have missed it, but figured the shooter would probably come his way. Tucson or Phoenix seemed the most likely destination for his getaway.

Jimmy opened the truck glove box and removed his Glock 21 and some foam earplugs. He ground one plug in each ear.

This could get tricky.

He turned Toby off so he could think. Then he stepped out of the truck, walked to the rear and bent his license plate up past horizontal. He got back in the truck and concentrated on the two-lane highway traffic as it whizzed by.

Six passenger cars.

Maybe he was making a mistake. He didn't have a dog in this fight, but there he was, ready to do battle. It's only a rifle.

One semi-truck.

This was Mike's thing, not his. Besides, they couldn't prove anything after fifty years, could they?

Four passenger cars.

What about the two dead guys? That was serious enough. This whole business mattered a lot to somebody.

Two Harleys.

Fifty years and they're still screwin' with us, thinking we're too helpless or too scared to do anything about it.

One UPS delivery truck.

They're dead wrong.

One Beige Hummer H2, driver, no passengers.

There you are, you magnificent bastard.

Jimmy started the big V8 and put it in gear. He let the Hummer get ahead before he pulled out and accelerated to

133

catch up, twin exhausts roaring.

He needed his quarry in the left lane. The Hummer moved to the left and passed a slow-moving truck, but then pulled back in the right lane. Jimmy rolled down his window and slid the Glock closer under his leg. He wiped the moisture from both palms.

Take your time.

He didn't have much time. It was only ten miles before they hit Tucson outskirts and heavier traffic. He needed to force the Hummer to pass him on the left. He hung back and watched. His chance came soon enough as traffic thinned. Jimmy pulled out and passed the Hummer and then got back in the right lane. When he was a half-mile ahead, he slowed to just below the speed limit.

The Hummer closed the gap behind him.

Jimmy eased up a little more.

The Hummer swung out to pass him on the left.

The driver didn't look at Jimmy, he just stared straight down the road. He was blonde with a crewcut, there was no doubt now. Jimmy matched speed until the Hummer's right rear tire was at his door. He steered with his knee and moved the Glock to the open window, holding tight with both hands. He only had one chance.

He'd only get one shot.

He took it.

CRACK!

The Hummer swerved right as its rear tire blew. Jimmy backed off the gas. The Hummer lurched into his lane, angling for the shoulder.

Now!

Jimmy nailed the throttle, the motor roared as his truck leaped.

He hit hard and stayed on the gas, pushing the Hummer ninety degrees around and off the road. Tires shuddered and howled in protest. The Hummer slid sideways at speed on the gravel shoulder, then slammed into a culvert and rolled once, twice.

Jimmy jumped on the brakes, finally stopping one-hundred feet beyond. Traffic on the highway slowed and gawked at the rollover.

Jimmy hopped out and jogged over. Dust shrouded the crash scene and slowly drifted to the ground. The Hummer dipped on bent suspension and flat tire, its body scraped and flattened on all sides.

The Hummer driver slumped forward in his seat, motionless but still strapped in. Blood trickled from a cut on his forehead. Jimmy checked, the man was breathing. Jimmy left him alone and went to work.

He tried to get a Hummer door opened. Nothing on the driver's side budged. He went around the other side, wiped some dirt off the glass and peered in the window.

A silver rifle case dominated the backend of the vehicle. It was the only thing he could see in the rear. Jimmy swore. What could he have done with it? He moved to another window.

There.

An old AR-15 was tucked behind the front seats. Jimmy jerked on the rear passenger door, once, twice, then it popped open. He grabbed the rifle and walked back to his pickup.

A trucker slowed and stopped his semi beside the scene. Cars pulled in behind the truck, several drivers got out and ran to the wreck.

Jimmy accelerated away, watching the turmoil shrink in his mirror. His hands shook when he took them off the wheel. This could have gone bad.

Real bad.

Miles clicked by. Jimmy's heart and breathing slowed to normal as he considered his next move.

He glanced at the rifle next to him. He'd taken a big risk, but it was worth the reward. The man deserved that much. Hell, America deserved that much.

Ask not, what your country can do for you…

***

Cole stood in the middle of the dirt road, watching the approaching cloud of dust. He shielded the sun with one hand, then relaxed when he saw it was the tow truck.

"I hope he brought some water," said Kate.

They decided against returning to the ranch for fear of upsetting June. Cole figured they made the mess and it should stay in their lap.

The driver pulled close and rolled down his window. "What happened?" he asked.

"Something went thru the radiator."

"You're lucky you reached me," the driver said. "It might have been tomorrow before somebody drove by. Nobody comes this far unless they're going to the Porter Ranch."

He maneuvered into position, dropped his hook and secured it underneath the Tahoe. When it was ready, Kate and Cole squeezed in the cab with the driver. He shared his water with them on the trip. They rode mostly in silence all the way to Willcox. Any energy they had earlier dissipated with the loss of the Kennedy rifle.

Cole received one call from Jimmy Stamps on the drive. They didn't talk long.

Kate asked, "What'd Jimmy say?"

"Not much, he said to meet him at the restaurant. He'll give us a ride home."

It was late afternoon when they pulled in the garage and Cole made storage arrangements.

"I'll probably have it towed up to Phoenix," he told them at Baxter's. Cole wanted the work done closer to home.

The manager looked out at the Tahoe. "I can give you a good price, let me figure it tight for you."

"Thanks, I'll call you tomorrow." Cole looked out the window, and across the street. "I'm supposed to meet a friend at Jake's. Is it far?"

"Two streets down at Main."

They carried their bags and walked to the restaurant. Once inside they looked for Jimmy. They found him waiting in a booth, eating a sandwich.

He waved them over. "What took you so long?"

"Tow truck was late. What's up?"

Jimmy filled them in on what happened with the Hummer and how he got the rifle back. Cole listened in disbelief.

"That's insane. This is getting out of hand."

"Yeah, well it's done," Jimmy said.

"Where is it?" Cole asked.

Jimmy moved to one side and exposed an object next to him. It was covered in black plastic and wrapped with silver duct tape.

Cole still couldn't believe it. "No police?"

"Not yet, anyway," Jimmy said, looking out the window. "Nobody got my plate."

"How's your truck?"

"It's wounded. They're pulling the bumper out and replacing one headlight. It'll get us home. Who was that guy?"

Cole waved one hand. "We don't know. We don't know anything. We don't know who he worked for. We don't know how he found us."

Jimmy didn't hesitate. "Transponder."

"I couldn't find it, but yeah, I'm sure they put a bug in my truck."

Kate leaned forward. "Who has that kind of equipment?"

"Professionals. Government. Organized crime."

"That still doesn't tell us anything. Except it's bigger than we thought."

She looked upset. "Maybe we should let this go. How many does that make—three dead, four dead?"

"What are you saying?"

"Maybe June is right," she said.

Jimmy looked at her. "Right about what?"

Cole said, "June Porter thinks the rifle is evil."

"So do I," Kate said

Jimmy scoffed. "That's crazy talk."

"Is it?" Kate asked. "Everyone involved with it is hurt or killed."

Cole relayed June's stories to Jimmy.

He didn't buy any of it. "It's a hunk of plastic and steel. It doesn't have a soul. It can only do what a man tells it to do."

"It's got a terrible history."

"That wasn't the rifle's decision," Jimmy said.

Kate protested. "Michael, you said a gun works with its owner or not. It can be a good gun or a bad gun."

He tried to stay out of it. "I didn't mean like this."

"Maybe the rifle wanted to kill Kennedy," she said. "Now it's killing us.

Jimmy's face said it all.

"What's it brought us in the last 24 hours?" she said.

"Ok, let's say you're right." Jimmy leaned forward, raising his voice. You're talkin' to a couple soldiers, here, lady. You can't just lay down, you gotta fight this thing, whatever the hell it is."

Cole tried to calm things down. "Look, it's over now. Let's just get home. If there's somebody else out there, they probably won't find us in Jimmy's truck."

Jimmy sat back in the seat and put his hands on the table. "Don't count on it. There's a lot of money at stake over this."

"Over what?"

"I read online there's supposed to be an auction on the fiftieth anniversary. They say the rifle's worth millions."

"To who?" Kate asked.

"Foreign dictators for one. I imagine Iran would love to have it. Imagine some Ayatollah wavin' it in the air, showin' it off on Al Jazeera."

Cole said, "Where'd you read about it?"

"Firearm forums."

They looked up as Baxter's garage mechanic walked in, his cap and shirt smeared with black grease. He came by their table, wiping his hands on a rag.

"Truck's ready, Jimmy. She ain't pretty but she's legal and safe. Sheet metal was rubbin' the front tire, I'd keep an eye on it."

"Thanks."

Jimmy got up to pay the bill, Cole stayed with the rifle.

"Let's take the freeway home," Cole said when he came back. "I'd rather not take the back roads. The freeway may be safer."

He said it, but he didn't believe it.

CHAPTER SIXTEEN

It was dark when they reached Cole's house and parked in the driveway. They lugged their bags and the rifle inside. Cole hid the rifle under his bed.

Jimmy turned on lights and pulled three water bottles from the refrigerator. They stood in the kitchen, drinking and staring at the floor.

Cole couldn't get the next task out of his mind; he needed to get it over with. Finally he put his bottle down. "I need to go talk to my sister."

"Now?" Kate asked.

"If I'm gonna sleep tonight, I need to talk to Susan—in person."

"You want my truck?" Jimmy asked.

"I'll take my car if the battery is up."

Cole opened the garage door and got in his 1975 Mustang fastback, a project car he hadn't driven in months. The paint was primered grey in several spots from weekend bodywork. It cranked over slowly, but rumbled to life. He pulled out and drove south.

He punched Susan's number as he drove, warning her that he was coming over. He wouldn't tell her why.

He thought about what he'd say and how she'd answer. He knew he'd get a fight.

They hadn't always been close, but she'd always been there for him. She taught him to drive at fifteen, taking him out on Arizona back roads, never yelling at his stupid mistakes. He paid her back by crashing her car when he shouldn't have been driving it. Forget it, she said. She even covered it up with their father.

She never got angry with him. Until lately, about JFK.

He stopped in front of Susan's house, all the lights were on. He sat and waited. His brain was ready but his feet were not. Finally he moved to her door.

She let him in with a curious glance. The house was quiet except for a murmur from the flat screen. Cole looked around for her husband.

"Where's Jim?"

"He took Billy to a ball game. What's going on?"

"I want to talk about dad."

She took him to her perfect living room. One peach upholstered couch with matching chair. One blonde coffee table, two matching side tables, two blue porcelain lamps. Her life seemed so different from his, so normal, sometimes they didn't seem related. Sometimes it surprised him they were siblings.

He slouched on her couch and rubbed his eyes, finally feeling the exhaustion. "What do you know about Dad in Dealey Plaza," he asked her.

"I know the same things you do. He was shot during the assassination."

"Yeah, I know that's what he said, and I believe him, but…"

"You have doubts," she said.

"I feel terrible about it, no one likes to think their father could lie, but some of it doesn't wash."

"Like what?"

"I've read all the reports from 1963, but nothing is ever mentioned about a spectator getting shot in Dealey," he said. "Just Kennedy."

"They thought he had a heart attack at first."

"Still, it would have been reported in a Dallas paper sometime."

"The story was JFK."

Cole shrugged. "You'd think it would be printed somewhere."

"He went to the Warren Commission about it, you know that."

"He said they didn't believe him. And I read the Warren Report."

She crossed her arms. "All of a sudden you don't believe him?"

"It's not that."

"They manipulated evidence. We don't have the whole story about what happened that day."

"You ever see any hospital reports?" he asked.

"No, but I've seen his scar," she said.

Cole nodded. "I've seen the scar too. But I've seen plenty of bullet hole scars. His doesn't look right."

"What's this about, Michael?"

"I've spent a lot of time and energy on this. I've risked my reputation. I've risked my life. I want to know it's all worth something."

She looked at him hard. "What happened down there?"

"It's not important," he said. "What's important is what happens now."

***

Jimmy wandered around the kitchen as Kate walked in. She crossed her arms and leaned against the Mexican-tile counter, watching him.

"You don't like me, do you Jimmy?"

He thought about that. "The jury's still out."

"I guess I've got to try harder."

Jimmy didn't answer.

She asked, "What's going on with Michael?"

"He's looking for the truth."

"About Dallas? He's got his truth; he's got the Kennedy rifle now."

"That's only half the truth." Jimmy examined the refrigerator, mystified how a man could live without beer. He searched the kitchen pantry and found a bag of pretzels; finally he spotted a sealed cardboard box of Corona on a lower shelf.

Warm beer. Worse than no beer.

"What's this got to do with his sister?"

"It's not his sister. It's his father."

"What about his father?"

"In Dealey Plaza," Jimmy said.

"I know a little, maybe you could fill me in."

"That probably oughta come from Mike." He scratched his belly. "I'm runnin' to the Jiffy Mart for some cold beer. You need anything?"

"Beer sounds good to me. Need any money?"

"I got it."

"Then I'm gonna jump in the shower while you guys are gone." She walked in the bedroom and closed the door.

Jimmy hesitated a moment in the living room, then went out to his truck.

***

Susan put one hand on her hip. "What do you mean, what happens now?"

Cole chose his words carefully. "I'd like your permission to exhume Dad's body."

Her head snapped up. "Why? Why would you want that?"

"I need to get an autopsy. I need to get the bullet still inside Dad."

"That's crazy." She picked a pack of cigarettes off the table, then threw them down. "Is this about JFK? No way."

"I have the rifle, Susan. I have the rifle that shot dad and shot Kennedy. The same rifle. We found it at the ranch were it was hidden in 1963."

"That's impossible."

"Kate got the information from her uncle; he was involved with the mob and the shooter. He's the one who had the rifle and hid it."

"Michael, are you sure?"

"I'd have to check the ballistics to be sure. The only way is to compare the rifling on the bullet."

"So you want to dig up dad over the stupid assassination?"

"It's not stupid, it's history. We need to show to the world. We have an obligation to the truth."

"An obligation?" She waved a hand. "Not mine. I can't give my permission for that. Don't ask me."

"Dad carried that bullet next to his heart for decades. Doctors said it was too close to risk removing it. Let it be for a good reason."

"And if you match the bullet, what will change? Will it make America a better place when everyone knows their leaders covered this up?"

"Most of them know that now."

"So it doesn't matter," she said.

"I use to think it didn't matter. But honesty is what makes America different. We need to tell the truth about that day."

"Some won't believe it anyway, even with your evidence. So there's no point."

"What about us? I need to see it myself, I need closure."

She looked away. "I'm sorry Michael. The cost is too high. I can't let you disturb his grave."

***

Robert Ryker hunched behind the wheel of his Avis rental and tried to get comfortable. Not even the strains of a Berlin Philharmonic Wagner Overture could sooth his mood—or his leg.

His limb ached from its old shrapnel wound, something he received delivering rifles to the Renamos rebels during the Mozambique civil war. The wound was an occupational hazard; one he hoped would not be necessary in the near future. One final sale was all he needed. One big sale. He moved his leg with two hands to a more comfortable position.

Ryker chose the darkest spot on the street to wait. He wasn't worried about the neighbors or the occasional car driving by. He could sit there and watch the house all night if necessary.

He wouldn't need to.

Headlights from an old pickup illuminated the front of Michael Cole's house as the truck pulled in the driveway. Two doors opened and three people got out. They pulled black bags from the rear bed and carried them inside.

Ryker kept one eye on the house and one eye on his Blackberry.

Ten minutes went past. The garage door came up and a car backed out, then it drove out of the subdivision. Ryker pulled the microphone from his ear and turned off Wagner. He picked the phone off the dash and held it in one hand, waiting.

The Blackberry slept.

Soon another man came out of the house, hopped in the pickup truck and drove away.

Minutes passed.

Ryker grew impatient, then worried. He opened the glove box to reveal a Walther P22. He reached for the gun, but stopped when his Blackberry buzzed.

CHAPTER SEVENTEEN

Cole drove slowly back to his house, struggling to come up with another solution. He should have known the outcome would be more dead ends, more confusion.

A riddle, wrapped in a mystery, surrounded by an enigma.

That was the only thing certain about the Kennedy assassination. Maybe that's all it ever would be. He had the rifle, but he couldn't prove it was in Dallas that day without his father's bullet and matching ballistics. He knew it was possible the bullet would be too damaged after hitting his father's rib, he wouldn't know until they removed it. Now, he'd never know.

The bullets that hit JFK had fragmented or disappeared. Even JFK's brain had vanished after it was transferred to Robert Kennedy. The bullet resting close to his father's heart was the only way to prove it. All he could do was establish the weapon *might have* been used by a knoll sniper. He could prove it was built in 1962 or 1963, he could show CIA connections, but that was the extent of it. It would be interesting reading for the conspiracy believers, but it would only bring him more ridicule.

He pulled in the driveway and waited on the garage door. He drove in and sat in the dark, his brain too-tired to think. He was out of ideas and out of energy. Finally he got out and entered the house.

Jimmy sat on the couch, resting his feet on the top of the rustic coffee table. Two open beer cans and his Glock 21 shared the table top.

"Any luck?" Jimmy asked.

Cole plopped down on the leather couch next to his friend. "Susan won't agree to an exhumation," he said. "She said it won't convince everyone, so why disturb our father's grave."

"She may be right," Jimmy said. "But it doesn't matter now."

Cole looked over. "Why?"

"Kate's gone. She took your Kennedy rifle."

"What!" Cole went in the bedroom and saw his clothes scattered on top of the bed. He dropped to his hands and knees and scanned underneath.

The rifle was gone.

He went back in the living room. "Where'd she go?"

Jimmy raised his hands. "Beats the hell out of me. I went out for twenty minutes to get some beer. When I came back she was gone. I'm sorry, Mike. I shouldn't have left the house."

"Damn it." Cole went back in the bedroom. "Her bag is gone."

"So is your duffle bag. She stuck the rifle in there and ran."

"Damn it." His stomach cramped at the loss.

Jimmy shook his head. "I fucked up big-time. I should have watched her."

"Was the door unlocked? Somebody must have taken her," Cole said.

"Somebody she called, maybe."

He hesitated. "You don't know that."

"So why'd she take her bag? Why take the time to put the rifle in your duffle?"

Cole ran his fingers thru his hair. *Think, Michael.* "She's probably still in the area."

"I drove all through the subdivision. She's gone, Mike. She's been playing you from the minute she walked in your door."

"I don't believe that."

"This whole thing's been a setup for you to find the rifle. She only needed you to make sure it was the right weapon."

"Why? What good would it do her to take it? All she wanted was the truth to come out."

"If that was true, they'd both still be here. Tell me about last night. Tell me you're not sleeping with her now."

"That's a different matter."

"No, it isn't. It just proves you been thinking with your dick." He shrugged. "Not that you're the first guy to do that."

Cole sat down, his mind racing. The betrayal was worse than the theft.

"Look at the facts," Jimmy said. "One day she shows up in your office with this story about the rifle. How'd Kate know about you?"

"From my book."

"But before she comes by, you get a lecture and a thumpin' from a couple low-lifes. Still you jump in with both feet."

Cole thought about it. "You're assuming she stole it. There's a chance somebody could have taken her and the rifle."

"There's no sign of that. It's over, Mike."

"Not yet."

Jimmy put his hand on Cole's shoulder. "Look, buddy. Before you push this thing any harder, you gotta decide if it's worth takin' a bullet. This is bigger than you and me."

He exhaled slowly. "Maybe. Probably."

"I don't mean to beat you up, but I'd hate to see you get in any deeper."

Cole couldn't imagine a deeper hole.

***

They drove in silence, the rifle sleeping on the rear seat of Ryker's rental Ford Taurus. Kate felt a mix of anger and relief. It was necessary, she told herself. It had to be this way.

They were on the freeway before she spoke.

"You didn't say anything about killing people." She didn't look at him. "I didn't sign up for that."

"Don't get wobbly on me now," Ryker said. "It's done."

She stared out her window at a blur of Phoenix lights. "Why?"

"Those idiots were a liability."

"They didn't know anything about the rifle."

"Loose ends. They'd been to Cole's office, I'm sure they left fingerprints. Those guys would have given us up in a minute."

"For what?"

"Murder. In case Michael Cole turned up dead."

"Leave Michael out of this." Her eyes flashed in the dark. "No more killing."

"This wouldn't have happened if you didn't try to go freelance on me. We need each other whether you like it or not."

She looked away. "Just for the record, I don't like it."

"We're a good partnership."

"I'm not your partner."

"Then think about the money."

She had been thinking about the money. It didn't comfort her.

Ryker asked. "Tell me about the shooter."

She told him what happened at Porter Ranch and Jimmy's retrieval of the rifle. She didn't mention her knowledge of the auction.

He chuckled at the stories. "We picked the right guy, didn't we?"

She didn't answer.

"This will just add to the mystique," he said.

"Who were they?"

"Had to be some spec-ops department trying to keep a lid on things. Like I said, just helps the legend."

"What now?" she asked.

"We need to get out of the state."

Kate looked back at the receding lights of Phoenix. "The airport's the other way."

He shifted behind the wheel. "I don't think we should fly out of Phoenix. I need to prepare the rifle for transport and it's too late for that. We can be in Albuquerque by morning. We'll split up there. But first I need gas."

Ryker pulled off the freeway and into a station. He got out of the car slowly and stood at the pump.

Kate sat, thinking of the mess she'd made of things. It was her fault, something she'd caused with bad choices. Bad choices had been a curse all her life. She sniffed, then looked in her purse for tissue. None. Her pockets. Nothing. She opened the vehicle glove box.

Another choice presented itself, this one in black steel and plastic. Maybe it wasn't a choice, she thought, but a solution.

When Ryker got back in, she was smiling.

"Thinking about the money, now?" he asked.

"Yes, actually," she said. "When do I get paid?"

"Sooner than we thought."

"You got a buyer?"

"Maybe. You'll get the rest, don't worry. All of it."

They drove out and back on the freeway.

"How are you going to prove it?"

"Prove what?"

"How can you prove it's the Kennedy rifle?"

"Don't worry about that, I've got connections," he said.

"To who?"

"To those who know."

They drove in silence, then Kate questioned him.

"Was it a Mafia hit?"

"Yes."

"Only the Mafia?"

"No," he said.

"Somebody told them to kill Kennedy?"

"Somebody paid Sam Giancana to make it happen."

"Who?"

"That's all I'm telling you."

"What about Oswald?"

"He didn't shoot the President."

"So he was a patsy after all."

"He was only at Dealey because his handler told him he was supposed to help stop an assassin."

"A CIA handler?"

"Oswald worked briefly for the CIA, starting at the Japanese U2 base. They had him send the Dallas FBI a note saying Kennedy was gonna be shot at the Trade Mart luncheon. So Hoover had a bunch of FBI agents there waiting and watching. When word came Kennedy was shot at Dealey, the FBI had to cover up their prior knowledge. It was a beautiful con."

"By who?"

"It's too dangerous, you don't want to know."

A mile clicked by, then Kate asked. "Why'd our government cover it up?"

Ryker paused. "Lyndon Johnson covered it up."

"That bastard."

"Like all of them. You gotta have enough money to insulate yourself from the bastards."

"How much money is that?"

"Whatever it is, I'm not there yet."

She thought. "And the rest of us peasants?"

"You've got to look out for yourself. That's what everybody else does."

Kate closed her eyes. She knew all about bastards, she drew them like flies. She was raised by one. She'd married one. She'd slept with plenty—until recently.

"Not everybody's a bastard," she said.

She put her head back on the headrest and tried to sleep, thinking of the night before.

Not everybody.

CHAPTER EIGHTEEN

Kate woke an hour later to see pine trees flashing by at the edge of the highway. Traffic had thinned, the road was down to two lanes. She touched her black window; it was cold to the touch. Minutes past, she didn't move. A highway sign lit up in their headlights, then disappeared as they sped by.

Flagstaff, 30 miles.

It was time.

She took deep breaths and steeled herself. She sat up in her seat and clutched her purse.

"I've got to pee," she said.

Ryker looked over. "Flagstaff's coming up."

"No, I mean now."

"There's nothing around here."

"I don't give a damn, all I need is a bush."

Ryker swore but pulled off at the next exit. Red cinders crunched under their tires as they stopped at the unpaved road crossing under their highway. Black forest wrapped all around them, unlit by civilization. "This work?" he asked.

"Perfect. I can drive for a while if you're tired," she said.

She got out with her purse and walked to the rear of the car. She pulled her panties down and squatted to relieve herself, then opened her purse and removed a snub-barrel .38 Smith and Wesson. She stood, fixed her wardrobe and walked to the driver's window. She tapped on it with her knuckle.

Ryker opened the window and spoke to her. "I'm fine. You can drive later."

She raised the pistol and pointed it at his face, two hands locked, just like her uncle taught her. "I'd rather drive now."

He stared like he'd never seen a revolver in his face. "What the hell are you doing?"

"Insulating myself from bastards, starting with you. Leave the keys, get out and walk away." She motioned with her gun.

Ryker glanced at the glove box.

"It's not there anymore," she said.

He opened the driver door and started to move.

"Don't forget your cane," she said.

He glared but came out with it. She backed out of his reach as he walked to the rear of the car.

"Farther."

He backed up, an outline in the dark. "What do you want?"

"More money. I know all about your little auction. I know what this rifle is worth. A hundred-grand is not nearly enough. I want a half-million."

"You are a crazy bitch."

She cocked her head. "Am I really? Then I want my hundred-thousand and the half-million. Six hundred thousand, when and how I tell you. Then you get the rifle."

He held up his hand. "Kate, don't be greedy. You're gonna screw up the whole thing."

"That's your problem." She walked to the driver's door. "I've got your little .22, I'm sure it has your fingerprints all over it. If anything happens to me or anything happens to Michael Cole, that pistol's going down to the Tucson

Sheriff along with your name. I'm sure they'd like to solve their shooting at Three-Points."

"Kate—" Ryker stepped forward, but stopped when she raised her gun.

"Shut up. You'll hear from me when I'm ready."

The rear tires spun as she drove off.

***

Cole checked his digital alarm clock again—two am. He put his head back on the pillow and watched the ceiling fan make slow, lazy circles over his bed. He listened to Jimmy snore in the other room, jealous of the big man's easy sleep.

Cole rolled out of bed and pulled on some Levi's, then walked to the kitchen. He yanked a bottle of Jack Daniel's from a lower cabinet and poured himself three fingers. He drank half the glass.

Where would she go?

That was a question with no answer. His other question was easier.

Should I follow her?

Let it go. Move on. It's not meant to be solved. It doesn't want to be solved.

He moved outside and sat on a lounge chair. Stars struggled to shine overhead, their distant efforts dimmed by Phoenix light pollution.

Nothing like the stars at Porter Ranch.

Cole took another drink. He'd gambled and lost. Without his father's bullet, it didn't matter anyway. It had all been a waste. He'd taken too many chances in search of the rifle. He'd put Jimmy at risk. He'd put Kate at risk.

No.

Kate put him at risk, he could accept that, now. How far would she have gone? Would she kill him over the rifle, over money? It had to be about the auction. How much was the rifle worth?

He had other questions, like who was Hummer Man? Who sent him? A government agency? That seemed unlikely. He was probably after the rifle for money, too.

Cole finished his drink and waited for the alcohol to numb his brain, to slow his thoughts. All he wanted was sleep; instead the whiskey glow took him back to Porter Ranch, back to Kate Marlowe's bed.

***

The Ford Taurus wandered as Kate's head drooped. It got halfway in the next lane before an angry horn snapped her awake. She reached over and turned the radio up until Gallup appeared twenty minutes later.

She found an all-night cafe right off the 10, warm and inviting. She locked the car doors and went inside to wake up and warm up. She sat at a window booth where she could watch her vehicle. A half-dozen patrons hunched at their tables, eating in silence.

"Coffee, please." Kate rubbed her hands together, wishing she'd packed warmer clothes.

When coffee arrived she ordered scrambled eggs. The blonde waitress looked like the woman in a picture on Kate's dresser, the one of her mother. It was Kate's only remnant of better times.

"Wait. Can I change that?" she asked the waitress. "Give me a fried egg and the short stack, please."

She held the coffee with both hands, the mug hovering under her nose as she inhaled the fresh-roast smell. She sipped and relaxed as the coffee's warmth spread through her body.

She smiled at the thought of Robert leaning on his cane in the dark, cursing a blue streak after her. What would he do now? What could the bastard do?

Nothing.

Police? Highway Patrol?

He couldn't. She had his little pistol. She had the rifle; he wouldn't risk losing the Kennedy rifle.

Six-hundred grand was cheap. He was probably getting ten-times that.

She could get someone at the firm to set up an account. Wilson would do it, he'd do anything if he thought he had a chance. A Cayman account for a direct wire transfer would be best, quick and quiet. Yes, the Caymans. Keep the money close by, hop over and visit it every now and then.

Some new clothes, low profile, not too many.

A new car, of course. Lose that wreck.

She looked out at her car in the lot, but all she could see was the outline, they'd turned off the overhead lights. She should have parked closer.

She needed to get rid of that rental car, the sooner the better. No way to explain an accident in Robert's rental. Albuquerque was another three hours, she could dump the Taurus at an airport lot and rent something else right there. She checked her watch. The timing was good; they'd be open by the time she rolled in.

She thought it would be better to drive all the way to Houston than fly with the rifle. Or she could ship it home and then fly, that was another possibility.

She couldn't think clearly.

Tired.

Guilt returned to ruin her mood. She should be happy; she was getting six-hundred thousand dollars.

Three hundred for selling her soul, three hundred for betraying a friend.

Toughen up.

She'd done a lot worse for a lot less. Why so melancholy?

She looked out at her car, and then breakfast arrived. She ate it all, surprised at how hungry she was. She got a coffee refill and drank until her eyes brightened.

She picked up the check and went to the register, then outside. Kate took a deep breath and a look at the sky. It was blacker and even colder. The lot had thinned, but a car sat close to her driver-side door. She squeezed between fenders and opened her purse for the keys.

Then she saw the glint of the blade.

One hand clutched the knife, the other slapped her purse. She fell down and her head bounced hard. The world was fuzzy black with streaks of light, then she was on her stomach. Gravel cut her cheek, but all she could think about was the gun, the gun in her purse, where was her purse?

Rays of light shone under the car, light so-far away, so blurry, so cold.

The gun.

Rough hands yanked at her shoes and her pants until gravel cut her bare knees. The knife pressed at her throat.

You scream, you die, it said through the blur.

She smelled its stink. She tasted her fear, but it was raw terror that froze her body. If she could only move her arms, if only she could reach it.

The gun.

Where was her gun?

The knife slipped under her panties and cut the thin cotton. Then they were gone and the blade was back to her neck. She recoiled from the sharp edge.

Now her brain heard strange words, long-forgotten words, words uttered softly from her own lips.

She was praying.
Please God, help me.
She was praying, something she hadn't done since a child. The words flowed easily, like they had never abandoned her.

She braced for the violation.

Instead she heard a noise. A noise from somewhere outside her head, loud yet close by.

Bells.

Bells ringing, over and over and over. Bells calling out when she could not.

"Hey you!"

It jumped up.

"Stop!"

Boots thudded on gravel and faded away in the darkness.

Kate heard one last bell, then a calming voice. A bearded angel in Kenworth cap and checkered flannel was at her side, soothing, caring, easing her fears. She sat up slowly. He helped her to her feet. His voice sounded soft but his arms felt strong.

He brought her shoes and pants, glancing away as she dressed. "Did he…" the angel asked.

She shook her head slowly. "No."

He didn't.

"You sure?"

He didn't.

"We should call the police."

"Please, just my purse."

He picked up her wallet and her phone and her pistol and put them in her purse, then handed it to her cautiously. "I heard the phone and I looked over and I saw him—are you sure you're all right?"

He didn't. The words wouldn't come.

"Your cheek is bleeding, and your lip. You should get checked out."

She touched the numb wetness on her face. "I'm fine."

The trucker gripped her arm and helped her to her driver's door. He stayed with her until she started her car and slowly pulled away, then watched until she was out of sight.

Kate drove two miles before she pulled off the highway. She turned around and looked at the back seat, staring at the Kennedy rifle shape in its black duffle bag. She jerked the door open and retched once, twice—then again until it was over. She closed the door.

Trembling hands brushed the hair from her face. She put her head back and inhaled deeply. Kate pulled her purse to her lap, removed her gun and put it between legs.

Bells.

She pulled her cell out and scrolled for the source. When she saw who, she covered her face with her hands.

Tears trickled until the sobs came.

***

The whiskey had worn off, but the Phoenix stars looked the same. Cole held the phone to his ear and let it ring over and over, but she never picked up. He didn't expect her to, but...

Ok.

He thought he could sleep now. He got off the lounge chair and went inside, grabbed his .45 off the kitchen counter and placed it on his nightstand, next to his pillow.

Just in case.

He lay down and closed his eyes, fading toward sleep. Minutes past, he drifted deeper, and then his eyes popped

wide open. He got up to retrieve his cell phone. He put it on the nightstand, next to his pillow, next to his gun.
Just in case.

CHAPTER NINETEEN

Cole's truck showed up three days later. They delivered it to a small repair shop in south Phoenix, someplace that wouldn't call the police when they found a fifty-caliber bullet in the engine block. Besides, the Chevy dealer would want to use all-new parts. At Cramer's place he could get a decent used motor from a salvage yard and a cheaper labor rate. Still, the labor cost was going to be horrendous.

So lack of money was reason Cole filled the slow leak in the Mustang's rear tire everyday instead of buying new rubber. His budget was shot for months.

Cole checked the car's air pressure with a tire gauge and then added a couple more pounds. He threw the hose back in his garage and drove off to work. When he got to Ballistic FX it was already after nine o'clock. He was surprised to see his sister parked out front. He apologized as they walked inside.

"No problem, I just got here. I was on the phone, anyway," Susan said.

He went to the refrigerator for water bottles. He handed her one as they sat on the couch. He hadn't talked to her since his visit and didn't know why she'd come.

"I hope you're not here to see the rifle," he said.

"No. Look, about the other night. I'm sorry I got angry with you."

"Forget it."

"I think I overreacted. I think if it's important to you, we should exhume Dad's body."

He didn't know what to say. "Why the change of heart?"

"I was selfish. I think it's something dad would've wanted. I mean, he did carry the bullet all these years."

"I know."

"You have the Kennedy rifle, but he has the Kennedy bullet."

"Yeah, well…"

She interrupted him. "I think he would be thrilled to do something important like this. The assassination meant a lot to him."

"It won't be necessary," he said.

She looked puzzled. "Why not? Really, it's fine with me. I can share some of the cost, I know it's expensive but…"

"I don't have it."

"Don't have what?" she asked.

"The rifle. Kate took it."

"She what?"

"Kate stole the rifle from me and left town. I don't know where it is."

She glared at him thru narrowed eyes. "I warned you about those redheads. Nobody listens to me."

"She doesn't have red hair, she's a blonde."

"Hah! That's even worse. Where'd she go?"

"I'm not sure. Probably Houston. That's where she lived."

She pondered that. "So, go get it. Jump on a plane, fly to Houston and get your rifle back."

He bounced off the couch and walked around the office. "No. I'm done. She'll have hidden it anyway, and I'm not gonna fight her for it. She needs it worse than I do, apparently."

"You're really giving it up? The whole crazy, Kennedy assassination, conspiracy nut, ruin your reputation thing? You're finally quitting?"

"I am," he said.

She watched him pacing back and forth.

"I reached my limit," he said. "Let them have the rifle, the grassy knoll, the whole damn thing. Whoever the hell they are. Stick a fork in me, mama, I'm done."

Cole sat back down. He'd said it.

She crossed her arms. "No," she finally said.

"No what?"

"No, you can't quit. You need to keep fighting. What would dad say?"

"Now you're crazy," he said.

"Think about it. You're so close; you had the rifle in your hands."

He didn't want to think about it anymore. He had been thinking and he'd reached his decision. "Finding the rifle was enough. I know what happened now, I'm content with that."

"Michael, I've never seen you quit anything. You need to go find Kate, find her and talk some sense into her. Heck, offer her money for it."

"Not gonna happen. First, I know she conned me just to find it. Besides, I think she already got her money for it."

"That bitch. You should talk to your friends at Phoenix PD, maybe they could call the Houston department, get her butt thrown in jail"

"Let it go. She's not a bad person."

Susan watched his face as he talked, then her tone softened. "You like her, don't you?"

He didn't answer.

"There's something there, Michael. I can see it."

He looked away. "We had something good. But something bad got in the way."

***

After Susan left, Cole tried to get things back to normal. He checked his email and answered the most pressing queries. There was good news. His client, Doctor Kyle had been acquitted, and Kyle referred Cole to another physician in similar need.

The next few months would be busy, he needed to get serious. Business had increased to the point he needed to hire some office help.

He set about composing a want ad for local posting. Qualifications? Must be more organized than the owner. That should be easy. Computer skills? Certainly better than his digitally-challenged existence. Did he want a male or a female employee? Male.

Can't put that.

A huge brown van honked once and stopped in front of his door. A UPS driver hopped out carrying a small box in one hand. Cole glanced at the driver's brown pants and shirt.

"Wearing your shorts already?" Cole asked.

The driver set the square box on the desk and handed Cole a clipboard. "It makes it easier to jog. I make more deliveries, I make more money."

Cole signed for the package and went back to work on his employment ad. Why couldn't he ask for a male assistant if he wanted one? He'd had enough women in his life for a while. Who decides all these rules, anyway? A person should be able to advertise for what he needed.

Wanted: Male assistant. Comfortable with Microsoft Excel, PowerPoint, dangerous hand tools and firearms. Not bothered by blood, an occasional F-bomb or shots of tequila consumed during business hours, as needed.

What's wrong with that?

He looked up when the UPS driver reappeared carrying another box under his arm.

"Sorry, Michael. Missed this one."

Cole signed again and the driver was off. Cole checked. He knew the small square box was numbered drill bits and safety glasses he'd ordered from McMaster, but the other was a surprise. He picked up the long box and looked at the label. It was from…

Albuquerque?

Cole used a razor knife to cut the cardboard, then pulled out a plastic bag followed by a cascade of packing foam.

It was the Kennedy rifle.

He dumped all the packing on the floor, searching the box for a note, a letter, anything that would tell him why. Nothing. Just the rifle. He checked the return address on the UPS shipping label. The box came from a simple pack and ship store in Albuquerque, New Mexico.

Why would she send it to him now?

A riddle. Wrapped in a mystery. Surrounded by an enigma.

He shouldn't have been surprised.

***

Cole took the rifle to the rear shop of Ballistic FX and set it on a metal work bench. He opened his tool box and started disassembly. In twenty minutes the bench was covered with major components and assemblies, cups of pins and small piles of springs. He cleaned and examined each part as it was removed.

He held the stainless steel barrel up to the light. The rifling, the 'twist' looked faster, tighter than the early Vietnam rifle barrels. Early barrels were one in fourteen twist, or the bullet made one complete turn in fourteen inches. The barrel Cole held was closer to one in ten inches. It would be more accurate with heavy bullets, more like a sniper's rifle barrel.

He knew the early AR15/M16's had a slow twist for a reason. A bullet left those barrels slightly unstable, wobbling like a badly-thrown football, even tumbling. When they hit their human target they made a larger wound-channel, more like a thirty-caliber than the .22 caliber they were.

He wasn't sure of the cartridge, though. It was probably a .223, but it could be a .222, like the very earliest rifles. He had to check it before he fired it, he didn't want it blowing up in his face.

He stuck the barrel in his wood-face vice, chamber up. Cole dug around in a drawer and came up with a piece of Cerrosafe alloy. He set an iron pan over a propane heater and dropped the soft metal in. While it was heating, Cole tamped a small piece of rag in the barrel chamber bore and coated the chamber walls with thin oil. When the Cerrosafe was fully melted, he carefully poured the liquid metal in the chamber.

It cooled quickly. He tapped the solid metal plug out with a long wooden dowel. Now he had an exact replica of the cartridge.

He pulled a loading manual off the shelf to get cartridge measurements. Then he scaled his replica with a digital caliber. *Yes.* It was indeed the .223, a standard rifle cartridge. He had a box of them waiting.

Cole cleaned the chamber and scrubbed the barrel, then reassembled the rifle. Tonight, he would fire it to retrieve a bullet from the rifle. He needed the bullet to compare rifling marks with the piece of lead in his dead father's chest.

***

After work, Cole took the time to vacuum his pool, figuring it might be hard to find a small caliber bullet among the many Mesquite leaves littering the pool bottom.

He stood at one end, planning to shoot toward his house and not the neighbor's in case of ricochet. Either way, he knew he was breaking the law. He'd considered using ballistic jelly to capture the bullet, but decided water would stop it unharmed.

He stood at one end of the pool and approximated the best angle. He fired.

Crack!

The bullet streaked through the water and came to rest on the pool bottom. He checked, it hadn't hit a wall. He put the rifle away and put on a swim suit. In ten minutes he was dry and holding the small missile in one hand, examining it closely.

Excellent.

He had half the puzzle solved. He opened a Corona to celebrate, but he wasn't out of the woods yet. The next step would be much tougher.

***

Grant Whelen woke to the sound of a monitor beeping overhead, then people talking close by. He concentrated, trying to understand the murmur of voices on the other side of the curtain surrounding his bed. He heard some Spanish, then some English. He opened his eyes and blinked.

Whelen placed one hand on the stainless steel bed rail and noticed an IV line taped to his arm. When he lifted his head off the pillow, he looked in the eyes of a man sitting on a chair at the foot of his bed. The man was grey-haired, muscular, with a curious facial scar. He was wearing a clean white shirt and a determined expression. It was not the nurse Whelen expected to see.

"How long have I been here?" Whelen asked

"Three days."

"Three days where?"

"University Medical Center."

Whelen racked his brain. It didn't register. "Where is that?"

"Tucson, Arizona. You're in the UofA Medical Center."

Tucson.

"I'm hungry."

"That's a good sign. I'll tell them."

Them?

Whelen raised his head again. "Who are you?"

"I told them I was your brother."

"My brother's not that ugly."

"My name is Robert Ryker."

Whelen put his head back on the pillow and stared at the ceiling. "Do I know you?"

"What do you remember?"

Whelen raised one hand and touched his forehead. "Car accident."

"Anything about a rifle?"

Whelen concentrated. *Shit.*

"The police will be asking you questions."

"That's what police do." Whelen lay quiet a minute, breathing deep. "Is there any water?"

Ryker reached for a cup with water and put a straw in it. He handed it to Whelen and talked while he sipped.

"They ran you off the road," Ryker said.

"No. My tire blew."

"They took the rifle."

Whelen closed his eyes, then looked at Ryker. "Who got it?"

"We can talk about it later."

"I'm not going anywhere."

"You will, sooner than you think. I've talked to your doctor. You were lucky."

Whelen pointed. "Did they leave my phone?"

"I don't see it. You from D.C.?" Ryker asked.

"You a policeman now?"

"Just a concerned citizen."

"I'm not your concern."

Ryker paused. "You're freelance, aren't you?"

"I'm a journalist."

"Of course you are."

"I work for the Murdoch News Corporation. I'm here doing a story on illegal immigrant trafficking."

Ryker smiled. "You should be out of here in two or three days. I'm staying in town. Come by and see me when you get out."

"Why should I do that?"

"I'll give you a half-million dollars if you do a job for me. Loews Ventana Resort. Robert Ryker. I'll leave the information at the hospital front desk in case you forget."

Then he left.

When Ryker was gone, Whelen considered the offer, then his stomach. He leaned on one elbow and buzzed for the nurse. He was hungry enough to eat hospital food.

CHAPTER TWENTY

Michael and Susan Cole arrived at Resthaven Cemetery fifteen minutes before ten am. The refrigerated truck was already there and the backhoe was in position, along with two workers holding shovels. A cemetery official in coat and tie was waiting for them.

"I'm Gabe Swanson," he said. "Do you have the permit?"

Cole handed him the certificate from the Attorney General's office.

He looked it over. "Fine. I've verified your father's grave site with public records. We're waiting on Maricopa County, then we can get started."

Cole nodded. "Thank you."

They walked down to the grave site, arriving at the same time as the county environmental health officer arrived.

Cole felt pangs of guilt when he saw their father's headstone.

"Are you sure?" he asked his sister.

"I'm positive. It's what dad would want," she said.

Swanson gave the go ahead and the backhoe took its first bite. Cole stepped close and took photos of each step of the process.

An hour later, the two men used their shovels to move the dirt closest to the casket. Another hour passed before they had it uncovered and prepared for removal. They snaked two wide nylon straps around the casket and winched it out. Gabe Swanson removed his jacket and stepped over the pile of dirt surrounding the grave. He examined the casket, looking closely for the name.

"Robert J. Cole," he read. "Alright. Proceed."

He walked over to Cole and Susan. "They'll get it wrapped up soon. I'm riding with the casket to the pathologist, of course. I'll verify the body's official chain of custody and give you the certificate. Are you two coming?"

"Yes," Michael said. "We want to be there each step of the way."

"We'll have the site ready for the reburial tomorrow. Please call us if there's any delay."

"We will."

Their pathologist, William Franklin, was using a medical facility in the middle of Phoenix. They followed the refrigerated truck to the clinic, then waited in the outer office for the results. They sat upright on cold metal chairs, staring at sterile green walls while the work went on in the back.

"How long will it take?" Susan asked.

"Couple hours, I'd guess. I asked them to get more photos."

"Gonna be gruesome. I know it's necessary for your authentication, but I don't want to see them."

Cole expressed his final misgivings. "I hope we're doing the right thing."

Susan put her hand on his arm. "You're worried you might be wrong, that's all. You've got a lot of years invested with this."

"I'm more worried that dad was wrong and it was some crazy story he made up that got out of hand."

"Dad could tell some whoppers, I'll give you that," she said. "But this story was true. He definitely had a bullet next to his heart, I've seen the x-rays."

Cole walked to the Pepsi machine and put in a dollar. He opened the soda but he only managed one sip before Doctor Franklin and Gabe Swanson entered the room wearing scrubs.

Cole and Susan looked at each other. It seemed too early for the results.

Doctor Franklin spoke. "Michael, your father died of a brain aneurism, correct?"

"Yes. It's on his death certificate. You have it there."

"Was an autopsy performed?"

"No, there was no reason. What's wrong?"

The doctor hesitated. "If you get scrubbed and suited up you can come back and see for yourself."

"I don't understand. See what?"

The doctor looked over at Susan, then back at Cole.

"Your father had post-mortem surgery performed on his thoracic cavity. His internal organs were surgically excised after his death. There's no heart. No lungs. No stomach. No liver. Certainly no bullet. Nothing.

"His chest cavity from trachea to duodenum is completely empty."

***

Grant Whelen drove past registration and check-in at Loews Ventana Canyon resort, then turned right at the tennis courts as Robert Ryker instructed. Casita number seven, he'd said. The casitas were individual units, built from the same rough-hewn beige block as the main resort.

The compact apartments seemed to sprout up from surrounding mounds of green ferns.

Whelen parked at Casita number five and walked the short distance on a winding brick path, surveying the area discreetly as he approached the carved-wood door at number seven. Ryker answered on the first knock and stood with cigar in hand.

"They let you smoke here?" Whelen asked.

"No. Bunch of tree-hugging bastards"

They moved inside and sat on overstuffed chairs covered with a simple Indian-motif design. Glass doors in the sitting area looked out on manicured fairways and a large chunk of Tucson below.

Ryker chewed on his unlit cigar. "How's the recovery?"

"Eighty percent. I move a little slower but the brain works fine." Whelen said. He moved his arms as if testing their function.

Ryker waved at the bar. "Join me for a scotch?"

"Dewars, if I have a choice."

Ryker rummaged through some mini bottles and then produced two glasses. He handed one to Whelen and drank half of his glass. Whelen didn't drink, he set it on the table in front of him.

"Thanks for coming," Ryker said.

"Don't thank me too soon," Whelen said. "I'm not comfortable with this yet. I'm not comfortable with you."

"I'm sure we know some of the same people."

"I doubt it. I don't know too many third-world dictators."

If Ryker was offended he didn't let on. "I was talking about Washington."

Whelen put his hands in his lap. "I'd rather you didn't."

"If you don't want to talk about D.C., I can give you Chicago references. I need a contractor who knows the weight of that rifle.

"Where is it?" Whelen asked.

"It's in Houston, my business partner has it."

"So why do you need me?"

"I don't trust her anymore; she's gone off the reservation."

"Her?"

"Kate Marlowe. We had a deal, she reneged and she's threatening to expose me. I want you to get the rifle from her and bring it to me in Maryland."

"I see."

"I'll pay you five-hundred thousand," Ryker said.

Whelen let that sink in. "You must want it bad."

"I can pay on delivery."

Whelen rubbed his neck. "How soon do you need this to happen?"

"Five or six days."

He considered. "What about your partner?"

"Dead is good enough."

Whelen stood and moved to the window to watch a golfer line up his putt. "I'm from a different generation. This whole Kennedy thing eludes me. What's all the hysteria about?"

Ryker stared at his cigar. "It's a moment in time when the curtain flew open and the world saw how sausage is made. Nobody liked it. Not the consumers or the producers."

"It's been half a century and it still stinks."

"America thought it was different. It turned out we're not much better than the rest of the world. Money brings power, power brings money."

"How much do you know about it?" Whelen asked.

"Everything," Ryker said.

Whelen turned. "Nobody knows everything. They know bits and pieces. They know the usual suspects."

"True."

"But you do?"

"Everything."

"Does your partner know too?"

"Ex-partner. Kate didn't need to know."

Whelen sat back down and adjusted his lightweight jacket. "I understand who benefited from Kennedy's death. I know who stepped aside and let it happen. I know who covered it up. But I don't know who ordered it."

Ryker smirked. "A side benefit from knowing the top arms dealers in the world."

"Who?"

"It's not who you'd expect."

"Just tell me. Who gave the official go ahead?"

Ryker leaned forward. "The Mossad."

"Bullshit."

"It's true. The Israelis were developing a nuclear bomb at their Dimona facility. Kennedy threatened to cut off America's support of Israel. He got in a huge pissing match with Ben-Gurion. Their conversations are still classified."

Whelen asked. "Who told you this?"

"Mossad has a gun-running arm headed by Amzi Dagan, we've worked together. He told me they sent a team to Montreal, then across to Chicago. The team paid the mob to do it so no Israeli would be caught at Dealey Plaza. But Mossad was there, watching."

"So the Prime Minister gave the go-ahead?"

Ryker nodded. "Ben-Gurion hated old Joe Kennedy, thought he worked with the Nazis in the thirties. Look what happened, they got the bomb after LBJ looked the other way. They were convinced they wouldn't survive without it. I think they were right."

"Amazing." Whelen nodded like he understood. Suddenly his arm moved in a blur and black steel appeared.

KACHUNK

Robert Ryker's left eye exploded as a subsonic nine-millimeter round passed through and entered his brain. The 147 grain bullet ricocheted twice inside Ryker's skull before coming to rest in the occipital lobe.

Whelen unscrewed the silencer from his Sig and put both pieces back under his jacket. He picked his glass of scotch up and drank it all, then put the glass in his jacket pocket.

He brought a hand towel from the bathroom and laid it respectfully over Ryker's face. Then he pulled on a pair of latex gloves and searched all three rooms. Satisfied with his anonymity, he removed his gloves and hung the Do Not Disturb sign on his way out.

Whelen walked to his car and drove out of the resort grounds. He was headed south toward the airport before he picked up his phone and called in his report.

"You were right, he knew...Marlowe? She doesn't know...I don't know where the hell the rifle is. Does it matter anymore?...Agreed, we're moving on. What's next...Dubai? The Saudi Prince I suppose... Damn it, Jensen. I need time off...Ok...Ok, warm her up. I'll be there in thirty minutes. I can sleep on the plane."

CHAPTER TWENTY-ONE

Cole landed at Houston Hobby with a one page map and an address. He rented a car at the airport and took the Tollway around to Hedwig Village. Kate's condo wasn't hard to find.

He didn't know what to expect, but he had to talk to her—if she'd see him. He hadn't slept much for weeks, he had to put it to bed, once and for all.

He rang her doorbell and waited.

Twice.

Three times.

He didn't expect her to be home. He knew she'd gone back to work, but maybe she'd moved her residence or was staying with friends. It wouldn't stop him. He'd confront her at work.

Cole turned around and walked back to his car. He had the key in the door when he heard her call.

"Michael!"

He turned and saw Kate in her condo doorway.

She let him in without a word. They sat on opposite couches.

Cole spoke first. "You changed your number."

She looked down at the floor. "It's not that I didn't want to talk to you. I should have called. I guess I was too ashamed."

He nodded. "Are you alright?"

"I'm fine."

Silence hung in the room.

"Why?" he asked.

"It's complicated."

"Then simplify it. I've got to know."

"Then ask me," she said.

"Why'd you send me the rifle?" he asked. "You went to so much trouble to sucker me out of it."

She winced at his words. "It's true, it started out that way. But then... things changed."

"I'm not here to beat you up about it. You had your reasons, I just want to know."

"Money," she said. "It was just money."

"So..." He looked at her and waited.

"In the end, it wasn't worth it."

"You must have been working with someone."

She nodded.

"The story about your uncle, was that true?"

"Of course."

"So why'd you need me?"

"To authenticate it. You were the best person for that."

"The best patsy, you mean. Like Oswald." He regretted it as soon as he said it.

"It wasn't what I wanted."

"I'm sorry, I'm just trying to get over it," Cole said. "What can you tell me?"

She spread her hands. "A guy approached me after my uncle's funeral. He said he was a collector, and he wanted to find the rifle used by the grassy knoll shooters. He knew my uncle's history, I don't know how."

"What's his name?"

"Robert. He wouldn't tell me his last name, he said that was best. He said if I helped him get the rifle, he'd give me fifty-thousand dollars."

Cole understood the temptation, but he couldn't forgive it. "What's this stuff about an auction?"

"I didn't know about that until Jimmy told us he'd seen it on the internet. When I found out what it was worth, I took the rifle for myself. I got greedy, I wanted more money." The guilt was all over her face. "I'm very sorry."

He nodded.

"What will you do with the rifle?" she asked.

"It's useless to me now," Cole said. "I had a bullet, or I thought I had a bullet, to place the rifle at Dealey Plaza. But it's gone."

"Gone?"

"They, whoever, took the evidence. There's no way to prove anything now, it's just an old rifle at this point. Not even the CIA will want it."

"It's worth something to someone, probably a lot."

"Not to me," he said. "Not without the matching bullet. I'll send the rifle back to you, if you want it."

Kate looked away. "It's evil. I don't want any part of it."

Cole waited a minute, and then asked. "What about us? Is there any part of us we can salvage?"

She looked back. "I'm not what you need, Michael. I'm bad news."

He got up and came over to her, then took her hand. "Maybe I should be the one to decide that."

"It would never work. Tell me the truth, could you ever completely trust me again?"

He didn't answer her.

"Without trust, there's no chance of us making it."

He nodded, finally letting his hope go. "I'm sorry it worked out this way."

"It's not your fault," she said. "I screwed it up. You and I, we worked for a while, let's leave it at that."

Some of the pain faded with the truth. He stood to leave. "You sure you're ok?"

"Don't worry about me. Take care of yourself." She walked him to the door.

He took her in his arms for one last kiss, then he walked away.

CHAPTER TWENTY-TWO

Cole thought his truck ran better than it did before it was wounded. Cramer did some tweaking with the exhaust and fuel delivery, along with a couple other tricks. Mileage and performance improved, even the repair bill was cheaper than the estimate.

Cole woke early to give it a good test run. He was east of Wickenburg, driving slowly along a dirt road deep in the central Arizona's old gold mine country. He hadn't been in this area since he was a teenager, but he knew exactly where he was going. When he saw Buckhorn Creek and the Bradshaw Mountain peaks line up, he stopped his truck at the side of the road.

He took his bag from the rear and slung it over his shoulder. He walked through clumps of yellow poppies dotting the black rock hill, checking alignment with the three peaks as he moved. Cole stepped carefully. He watched for rattlesnakes, not wanting to be struck this far from civilization.

He stopped to get his bearings, thinking it was tough to judge with all the new desert greenery. Finally he found the mine opening, still covered with lumber and guarded by a faded warning sign.

DANGER!
ABANDONED
MINE SHAFT

He sat down and pulled a framing hammer from his bag and pried off the boards covering the entrance.

Cole dropped a stone through the gap and listened. Satisfied, he pulled the Kennedy rifle out of the bag and held it suspended over the vertical shaft. He paused a moment, then he let it fall. Seconds past, and then he heard a faint clatter and a thud far below. Cole rose and picked up the biggest stones from the area he could carry and dropped them down the shaft. He listened to the satisfying crunch below as they smashed the rifle.

It was as satisfying as putting a stake in the damn thing's heart.

He didn't want it sitting on someone's shelf or on display somewhere as a trophy. He saw that evil can lay dormant, waiting for the right sole to falter. If it lived, someday the Kennedy rifle might come back to life. He couldn't live with that. The rifle had caused enough destruction already, taken enough lives, just by its existence.

He nailed the old boards back on the mine opening and walked back to his truck.

It took almost three hours to get back to Ballistic FX. He didn't mind the drive. He thought about his father on the trip. He'd been right about Dealey Plaza all along, now Cole knew that. He accepted his father couldn't change anything in the aftermath of Dallas, any more than Cole could change anything now. His father was just one man against the machine, just like his son.

With decades of doubt and frustration behind him, Cole felt fresh and energized. He could get on with his life, what ever that might be. Even the traffic cooperated all the way to Scottsdale.

When he arrived at work, he saw a woman in black slacks and blue silk blouse waiting at his front door. She appeared slender at first glance, thin with an extra ten pounds—in the right places.

He pulled in the space directly in front his shop and stepped out.

"Hello," he said to her. "I'm Michael Cole."

She turned around and smiled warmly. Thirty-five maybe.

He unlocked the front door and let her in.

"I'm here about your ad," she said. "The office assistant?"

"Yes, I'm sorry, I thought that started tomorrow. Please, sit down."

She brushed some brunette locks from her face while he looked over her resume.

Sonia Tomei.

"You certainly have the computer skills we need," Cole said. "And I see some office management experience."

"Six years," she said. "I quit two months ago, after going through a divorce. I moved out here for a fresh start. You know, the usual story."

He glanced again at her resume.

Brooklyn, New York.

Cole thought he should address his hesitation right away. "Do you have a problem with guns?"

She paused. "I'm not sure what you mean. I don't own one, if that's what you're asking."

"I see you moved here from New York. I know some easterners aren't comfortable with guns. I work with firearms here, and I carry a gun everyday."

"A loaded gun?" she asked.

He smiled politely. "If it wasn't loaded, I'd have to call it something else."

She swept her hair back with one hand and looked at him through soft brown eyes. "To tell you the truth, I wouldn't know a shotgun from a rifle. And all these handguns make me nervous. They're incredibly loud, they go off unexpectedly and people die. I don't like them."

"I see." Cole put her resume down and looked at his watch. "Well. I just thought you might own one for self-defense. I know New York can be a tough place, but I understand they're illegal there."

She gripped the purse in her lap. "Oh yeah, they're illegal. But everyone I know has one. It's just me and guns. You see…"

She pulled a hand from her purse and casually flipped her wrist. Cole glimpsed bright-red fingernails and a wicked curved-steel blade.

"I don't get this whole gun business," she said. "But knives I understand."

She smiled, folded the knife and put it back in her purse.

Cole straightened-up in his chair. "So, Sonia. When can you start?"

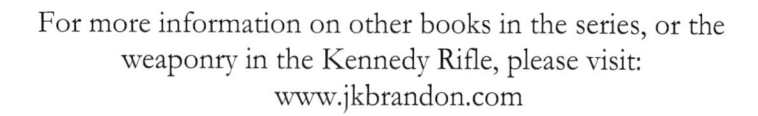

For more information on other books in the series, or the weaponry in the Kennedy Rifle, please visit:
www.jkbrandon.com

Catch Michael Cole and Sonia Tomei in their follow-up thriller, *The Steel Violin*.

The Steel Violin
EXCERPT

JK Brandon

CHAPTER ONE

If anything grabbed Michael Cole's attention, it was precision firearms and beautiful redheads. His morning started with a blatant seduction attempt by both. Cole struggled to resist, but he was intrigued by the aromatic mix of Chanel No.5 and Hoppes No.9.

He examined the black rifle sitting on his mahogany desk. Inside his little office, the massive weapon looked intimidating, but then so did she.

Still...

"I'm afraid I can't help you," he said.

The redhead leaned forward in her chair. "Please, Mister Cole. You must. You have to."

Normally he'd be all in by now—a beautiful woman in trouble, a sniper rifle and a murder—but there was a glitch.

"You said you were bringing me a murder weapon, but nobody's been killed. I can't see the problem, or how I can help."

She sighed. "That's what the police said."

Cole lugged the rifle in from her silver Jaguar sedan.

Robyn Daggett Trent was about thirty, petite and probably a bit warm in her ankle-length black linen skirt. It was August in Phoenix. Her makeup was subtle but her dazzling red hair stood out, all teased and tousled and a bit out of place. It was not his normal morning. Gorgeous redheads were rare enough, much-less one accessorized with a bolt-action rifle.

"How'd you hear about Ballistic FX?" he asked.

"One of the deputies told me, I didn't get his name. Off the record, he said, Michael Cole might be able to help you."

"Was he joking?"

"No, he was serious. Why?" she said.

"I don't get many local referrals."

"That's what you do here, gun stuff, right?"

Cole had an easy grin and eyes that smiled when he did. "Gun stuff is pretty accurate. I offer court-certified expert testimony on firearms and ballistics. I also do firearm analysis."

"That's what I need, analysis."

He hoped she wasn't talking about psychiatric.

Robyn Trent was old Arizona money, one of the Daggetts, a well-known Phoenix family that sold their mile of Camelback Road real-estate six months before the crash.

Cole put his hand on the rifle stock. "You said it was in the back of a rental car?"

She nodded. "It looked like the driver slid off our gravel road and hiked out for help. Aurelio—that's our foreman—he found it first and searched the trunk."

That gave Cole pause. "Wouldn't he have to break in, why would he do that?"

"It was on the private road to our ranch and I think Aurelio got suspicious."

"Have you had trouble before?"

"A little." She didn't elaborate. "Anyway, no one ever came to get the car. With this thing in the back, I can see why."

Cole studied the rifle resting on its steel bipod. It was production piece made by Accuracy International, an AX model with a folding stock. Even with its 27 inch barrel and muzzle break, it would shorten enough to conceal and transport easily.

"It is unusual, I'll give you that. But I imagine you're worried about something more serious than a lost rifle."

"I think someone planned to kill my husband."

She seemed very sure about that.

Cole took a closer look at the rifle. He opened the bolt, slid it out of the receiver and examined the bolt face. It was huge, magnum or super magnum—definitely long range. "You find any cartridges in the car?"

"Any what?"

"Bullets."

"Oh yes, a little box." She dug in her purse and produced a plastic container about four-inches square.

"There's six."

Cole opened the container and removed one cartridge. They were .338 Lapua Magnum, a specialty sniper chambering. He thought maybe Thomas Trent should be concerned, this was not a lost deer rifle.

"Why didn't your husband come with you?"

She studied the webbing on her Gucci purse, searching for flaws—or the truth. "He doesn't know I'm here, he didn't want me to take it any further. He didn't even want me to go to the police, but I insisted. He said he doesn't want the bad publicity."

"Why would someone want to kill your husband?"

"It's probably about his business. He runs a mutual fund—Benchmark Global, have you heard of it?"

"Sorry. Never was very good at investing." That was one reason Cole considered taking the job.

"I get the drift there's been something going on at work, a wife can tell, you know. He's been despondent, distant for months, but he won't talk about it."

"Would he talk to me about this?" Cole asked.

"Probably not, Thomas is very stubborn."

Cole slid the cartridge back into the plastic case. "I'm sorry, but this is a little out of my line. I don't see how I can help if your husband won't cooperate."

Robyn Trent moved forward and placed her hand on Cole's arm. Her silk blouse fell open to reveal an immodest amount of creamy-white skin. "Please, Mr. Cole, I really need your help."

"AHEM."

Cole turned to see a familiar face and a familiar pose, arms folded across her chest as she leaned in the doorway. She shot Robyn Trent a look that had to melt her pantyhose.

"I'm back," she announced. "Just in time, it would seem."

Brunette confronts redhead.

Cole grinned. "Sonia Tomei, this is Robyn Trent, she's hoping to engage my services."

"Yeah. I see that," Sonia said.

"Miss Tomei is my invaluable assistant," Cole said.

Robyn Trent acknowledged Sonia's presence but not much more. "How nice." She turned back to Cole and smiled, pantyhose intact.

Redhead rebuffs brunette.

"I'll be out here if you need any help." Sonia retreated to her front office, shuffling paper and slamming the furniture.

Cole returned to his immediate problem. "Did anyone try to trace the rental car?"

"Yes, but the police said the renter used an alias. You'd think that alone would interest them. They must think it's useless, they kind of put me off."

"You were at the ranch that day?"

"I drove up that morning, we live in town during the week, Scottsdale."

"Was your husband up there?"

"He was due to arrive that evening. It was Friday, he flies his Piper in every Friday afternoon if the weather is good. He says he needs the stick time, and it's a good release after wrestling the market all week."

"Flies in from where?"

"Sky Harbor. The Benchmark headquarters is in downtown Phoenix; he feels he does better away from Wall Street, away from all the hype. At the end of the week we go to the Carefree ranch to decompress."

The little town of Carefree was an hour north of Phoenix, cooler in temperature, higher in altitude and much-higher in real estate values. It was one of those Arizona places that were beautiful until everybody moved there.

"Then you're just east of there? Cole asked. "Those skyranches?"

"Actually it's further north, I can draw you a map. Does this mean you'll do it?"

He didn't think so. He hated dealing with rich clients and their haughty attitudes. He had the Bronson trial testimony coming up—but that was a month away and his investigation was already done. He had the time. The problem was, there was something about this job that reminded him of a bad experience.

He glanced out his door in Sonia's direction, wondering what she thought of this. She noticed him looking and glared back from behind her computer screen.

Never mind.

Murder weapon, but no murder. Something didn't seem right, he better not get involved. Just before he told her, Robyn opened her high-dollar purse, withdrew a check and slid it across the table.

He held up a hand in protest. Then he glanced down at the amount.

***

After she drove off, Cole ventured out to test the weather in the front office. When Sonia saw him she pulled her blouse out in exaggerated points. "Oh, Mr. Cole," she breathed, "you must help me." She blinked her eyelashes. "I can't find my rear-end."

He grinned. "I could probably help her with that."

Sonia leaned back in her chair. "Did you fall for that helpless female act?"

Cole held up the check for her to see. "Five grand. Up front."

Sonia's face dropped.

"Don't worry, she's married," he said.

Sonia took the check, looked at the amount and put in her pencil drawer. "I'm telling you, she's trouble. Any idiot could see that."

"I'm not just any idiot."

"That's true."

Cole resisted getting involved with Sonia, but it was a constant battle for him. She was just what he needed, so he kept her at arm's length. It wasn't easy.

Sonia was tall, about two-thirds legs and the rest attitude. Cole wasn't sure what had attracted him first. Feisty, intelligent, sensual—what more could a guy want?

Less feisty.

"So what's her problem?" she asked.

"She thinks someone is hunting her husband. Where's my chocolate donut?"

Sonia handed him a small white bag. "I got you a bran muffin."

He held it at arm's length. "It's not enough you're trying to improve my personality, now you're meddling with my colon. I asked for a chocolate donut."

"They were out."

"That gives you a clue to their relative worth. They're out of chocolate donuts, but they have plenty of bran muffins. There's a reason."

"True. Men care more about taste than lifespan."

"Cancer's not my karma, I'm more likely to die of a bullet wound." he said.

"Probably. But no jury would ever convict me." Sonia sipped her coffee. "That's what the rifle's about, someone shot at her husband?"

"No shots were fired. They found it on her property, their ranch up north. It was left in the trunk of a rental car. Sheriff won't investigate any further, she wants me to trace it, see where it came from."

"Who's her husband?"

"Thomas Trent."

Sonia turned. "The mutual fund guy? Benchmark Global Growth?"

"You heard of him?" Cole was impressed.

"He's Arizona's claim to fame. Their fund is up a hundred percent for the year. Don't you listen to business news?"

"In a word? I suppose you put all your money in stocks."

"Quite a bit, at least the meager amount of pay I have left after my bills."

He ignored the dig. "You might want to consider some bank CDs for a while, if Robyn's right about his future."

"Oh, it's Robyn, now. Miss try-too-hard."

The only problem with Robyn Trent was Cole's big mouth. One time he'd admitted to Sonia he had a thing for redheads, one of those rare moments when men do stupid things.

He tried to backtrack. "Redheads are like the convertible in the showroom window. They attract a lot of attention, but men always buy the four-door sedan brunette."

She softened. "Be careful of test drives."

He took her hand. "I think the older models are better, even if they're a little used."

Sonia stood and moved very close, then spoke softly. "So, that's what you think of me? Your invaluable assistant? Used car?"

He hesitated. "Pre-owned?"

Sonia grabbed the company checkbook and the Trent check and walked toward the door. "I'm gonna hammer this check. Maybe I'll get my hair dyed red."

She muttered as she walked. "Used car."

He called after her. "Low mileage, though."

It didn't help.

***

Cole finished his snack and returned to take a closer look at the rifle. He carried it to his shop in the rear of Ballistic FX and set it on the wood-topped workbench in the center of the room.

The rifle had everything a well-dressed sniper demanded. Adjustable buttplate and cheekpiece, full-length scope rail, attached bipod and monopod. All it needed was ammunition. Why would anyone leave it in the trunk of a car? What kind of assassin was that incompetent?

He drank some coffee and thought about that. Maybe the owner was forced to leave it to avoid being seen, and planned to get back before it was discovered.

Cole paused, something about the weapon looked off. He examined the barrel closer. It had a different finish than the rest of the black rifle, and a hand-applied caliber stamping. A replacement, he though. The rifle looked new, so the barrel couldn't have worn out. A gunsmith had modified a major rifle component on a brand-new rifle, but for what reason?

Quality? Diameter? Twist?

Cole threaded a white cotton patch on his cleaning rod and inserted it in the muzzle. Using an inspection light, he pushed and watched the revolution of the patch, marking then measuring the rod's movement. He repeated the procedure three times, but it never seemed correct. The twist came out one in eight, or one complete turn of the barrel rifling every eight inches—extremely fast.

For a .338 caliber?

That was the wrong barrel spec, it made no sense.

A buzzer went off and Cole knew someone had entered the outer office. He glanced at his watch, it was probably Sonia. He took his coffee and went to check.

It wasn't Sonia, it was two gentlemen, at least they were dressed the part. Probably sales, he thought. Positioned as it was in a Scottsdale Industrial Park, Cole's business got its share of persistent salesmen. No solicitor worth his salt obeyed the 'No Solicitors' sign on the front door. He couldn't really blame them.

They didn't look like typical salesmen, although the tall one carried a briefcase under his arm. He looked in such good shape he could have been selling health-club memberships, but the other looked squat and a bit rough around the edges.

"Can I help you?" Cole asked.

"I'm sure you can." The short guy examined the rows of plaques on the walls of the office, then pointed at them. "Are these your awards?"

The plaques were from Cole's years in benchrest shooting.

"Yes."

"You must be a good shot."

Cole shrugged.

"You work on firearms here?" he asked.

He spoke with an accent, but Cole couldn't place it.

"No. We do analysis, testing, identification." That was only a partial list, but many people wandered in looking for gunsmithing or repair. "Are you looking for a gunsmith?" Cole asked.

Short guy acted like he didn't hear the question. "Analysis and identification. I see. Then you should know a lot about firearms, Mister..."

"Cole. Michael Cole." He switched his cautionary mode to condition yellow. He carried his pistol behind his hip. "Firearms and ballistics."

"You know automatics?" short guy asked.

"I do."

Short guy pointed back at the second gentlemen without taking his eyes off Cole. "Then you might know about briefcase-mounted HK my friend has pointed at your chest."

Cole knew. When he looked closely he could see the small black hole in the edge of the special briefcase where the barrel lurked, pointing directly at him. Cole nodded slowly. "MP-5K. Navy model, 9-mm. Thirty-round magazine."

This was not his normal morning, indeed.

"If you move your hands, my friend will shoot you. He's a very good shot, too."

"Got it."

The short guy turned and walked to the door and locked it, then lowered the window shades on the three front windows.

Cole could draw and fire his .45 in one second, but in that same second the HK sub-machine gun could spit thirteen bullets. Assuming, of course, the shooter had any reaction time at all. Cole assumed he did. He waited, hands motionless, eyes on briefcase. A good man knows his limitations.

Short guy returned. "Put hands on head...slowly...now go over and lean against the wall, palms flat."

Cole spread and leaned, he knew the drill, he'd spent years with the Phoenix Police Department. Somehow he didn't think these gentlemen had ever been on a police force. He pictured them more as the leanees. "What do you want?"

No answer.

Rude, too.

The short guy kicked Cole's feet a little further away from the wall, then yanked Cole's pistol out of his holster and looked it over. "Colt 1911 .45 ACP. See, I know a little about firearms myself." He looked at it again. "Cocked and locked, this is some serious weapon."

He dropped the pistol's magazine and looked at the round on top. "Federal Hydroshock. Serious ammo. You are serious guy, Mr. Cole. But right now you're in serious trouble." He slipped the magazine in his pocket. "But we still got one in the chamber, don't we? That's all you .45 guys think you need, right? One big bullet?" He put the barrel against Cole's temple and clicked the safety off.

It was the loudest sound Cole had ever heard.

"Right. One in the chamber," Cole repeated, just in case the guy forgot. Cole's palms sweat into the office wall, but he worried more about Sonia returning from the bank than losing his brains.

"That's right. Now where is rifle Mrs. Trent was kind enough to drop off for us?"

Of course.

"It's in the back."

"Alex, check it out."

Alex walked to the back office. He hadn't said one word yet but he was one hell of a communicator. He returned with the Accuracy International rifle and stood it in the corner by the door.

Short guy waited until his friend resumed his position as covert sub-gunner, then he took the .45 off Cole's skull. "It would be embarrassing to be shot with your own gun, don't you think?"

Not to mention painful.

"We don't like people investigating our business," he said.

"What business is that?" Cole asked.

"Now see, I get the feeling you don't understand our problem." The short guy stood close to Cole and slapped the pistol against his palm. Terrible gun safety.

"Careful," Cole said, "that's a three-pound trigger. *Ooof!*" Cole dropped to his knees from the fist to his ribs.

"Get up."

Cole struggled to his feet.

"Listen wise guy. Right now *you* are the problem. You know what IRA does to problem people?"

"Talks 'em to death?"

Short guy jabbed the muzzle into the soft backside of Cole's leg, right behind his knee. "They kneecap 'em."

Suddenly Cole didn't feel much like a wise guy. He preferred his bullets in the head.

"How tough are you, Mr. Cole?"

Cole gritted his teeth and waited to find out.

"Let's think about this first." Shorty twisted the barrel back and forth. "Forty-five caliber ACP. Big hole going in, very-big hole going out. But you're the ballistics expert, you already know that, don't you."

"Yeah." Cole was sweating serious now, his leg twitched at the press of the muzzle.

"Imagine a big hole in your kneecap. Imagine how painful it will be. Imagine dragging this useless piece of meat around for the next fifty years. That's if you're lucky, they'll probably cut the mess off."

"Uhmm."

"Maybe they won't need to; maybe you will bleed to death before you get help. Imagine that for a moment."

Cole imagined.

It was a long moment.

Made in the USA
Lexington, KY
09 April 2012